THE EX FACTOR

HARINI SRINIVASAN is the author of a historical detective novel, *The Curse of Anuganga*, the novellas *Ek Confusing Love Story* and *Death at Arcade Emporia*, a children's book, *The Wizard Tales: Adventures of Bun-Bun*, and several short stories. A former civil servant, she is an editor and a content management professional by day, and an author by night. She can be found multitasking most of the time. An aficionado of old Hindi cinema, she lives in Gurugram with her family.

THE EX FACTOR

Harini Srinivasan

Om Books International

First published in 2023 by

Om Books International

Corporate & Editorial Office
A-12, Sector 64, Noida 201 301
Uttar Pradesh, India
Phone: +91 120 477 4100
Email: editorial@ombooks.com
Website: www.ombooksinternational.com

Sales Office
107, Ansari Road, Darya Ganj,
New Delhi 110 002, India
Phone: +91 11 4000 9000
Email: sales@ombooks.com
Website: www.ombooks.com

ISBN: 978-93-5376-857-7

Printed in India

10 9 8 7 6 5 4 3 2 1

To Aikantika Das, my sweet,
spunky friend and ex-colleague

1

Everything that could go wrong, went wrong today. Every single thing.

It all started at some unearthly hour in the morning. I could hear my mother's voice go on and on about something in a rather high-pitched tone. I tried to sleep, roll over to the other side and close my ears but to no avail. She was simply too loud and clearly too distraught. My father, ever taciturn and unflappable, was muttering something, probably to assure her and calm her down. I got up, now fully awake and dragged myself down to the scene of all this action—the floor below.

There stood Ma in front of the kitchen, flailing her arms, waving two phones (*Oh holy fuck. One of them is mine. How on earth did she get it? Was it not under my pillow? Has she seen my messages? Oh no*). *Wait, why is she shouting? Has she found out that her daughter certainly is not as shareef as she looks?* Choco and Chipki, our two dogs were watching her, what seemed to be in absolute awe. Well, the way Ma was shrieking (at the phone) was much louder than their combined barking, which is a big thing, mind you. You see, our maid ran away two days back, not willing to work anymore in this mad Bengali household, where everyone from the master to the dogs was definitely crazy. And just for your information, she was a Bengali too!

As I watched with absolute horror (and part fascination), I figured out what the matter was. The cook had taken off. Without notice! All phones available in the house had been employed to see whether she would answer and could be located, but in vain.

To us, in the Roy household, this was nothing short of a tragedy. First the maid, and now the cook. What were we going to do? What was I going to do? As I grappled with this changed reality, I realised that the shrieking had stopped and Ma and Baba were now looking at me – with that ominous look which said – *Lady, get started*!

Ever since the maid had absconded, it had fallen upon me to take Choco and Chipki out for their morning walks—an activity which per se should not be so taxing. I love my dogs and they love me, period. However, due to certain extraneous circumstances, this normal activity was one that unfortunately required much strategizing—both Baba and I had come up with an extensive plan. As I braced myself to go ahead with that plan, it struck me that my life was fucked up now. Other than walking these two dogs, which was followed by my daily gym schedule and then work, I would probably have to prepare some kind of breakfast. Ma was already busy cooking chicken for her babies (I mean the dogs); I did not think the favour would be extended to me—a grown 25-year-old working professional (*albeit, in my first job, but still*...) who lived with her parents, much to my friends' consternation. Ma and Baba were both civil servants working with different ministries, holding important portfolios. They simply did not have the time or inclination to mollycoddle me.

So, the morning started, with me getting dragged out of bed to drag the dogs to do their *tatti*, following which, the day got progressively worse. As I was being dragged by the dogs, my phone beeped.

It was a message from Hawkeye, my boss. "Check your e-mail and call me." Even though his name is fairly innocuous and common, all over the place 'Rahul', he was hardly that—innocuous I mean. He was annoying and dangerous, like a falcon hunting its prey. Falcons were probably less annoying.

Rahul Dewan usually entered the office with a slow and purposeful gait, scanning the area with his hawk-like eyes to look for any tell-tale signs. And if I was goofing off (which in his dictionary meant anything other than squinting at the computer screen with an annoyed, shitty expression), he would descend upon me and shoot an entire list of to-do items that I was supposed to complete half an hour back! *More about this particular form of torture for later.*

As for that moment, when Choco and Chipki were deciding to run in two separate directions, my only focus, other than deciding which direction I should let myself be pulled in, was to deal with Hawkeye's e-mail. He had some fuck-all important meeting at 10:00, and he required some information for that within half an hour. *Half an hour? Is he nuts?* It was not possible. As I composed a perfectly dignified reply to Hawkeye in my mind, absolute mayhem ensued around me. Chipki, our lovely Indian stray (brought home from the streets by yours truly in a moment of utter insanity), was barking like there was no tomorrow or even today, and was pulling me towards my left with all her might. And of course, she won! Choco, our lovely labrador, gentle and sweet, was barking too and was more eager to move to the right. It was then that I saw the reason behind this mayhem. My neighbour's Indian dog, Makkhan Singh, was coming our way, on his morning walk. Remember the strategizing I mentioned earlier? Makkhan Singh's presence on the ground floor was the reason for this. Chipki, territorial, fierce and plain *khadoos*, did not like Makkhan Singh while Choco loved him. To avoid absolute drama early in the morning, Baba and I took a dog each and went in opposite directions, all to divert Makkhan's attention and spare our lives. Today Baba had stayed back to take stock of the domestic crisis, which probably meant making frantic calls to whoever picked up the phone at this unearthly hour, to seek a maid and a cook. Hence, I had been left to fend off these three witches … no … bitches … err whatever you may call a combo of one dog and two bitches. Fend them off I did, somehow and navigated my way back home. Finally.

***

"Rahul, *haan* sorry, I just saw your e-mail. *Accha*, but I don't think I will be able to give you all this information by 9:30. Analysis *run karne mein* time *lagta hai*."

"Oindrilla, *he he he*, but this has to be done, *he he he*…"

Did I mention Hawkeye has a particularly menacing laugh? Nasal and shrill – a laugh that had merely been irritating at one point in time, had assumed a menacing quality ever since he became my supervisor. His laugh did the trick. I would rather not listen to that! Working on that fuck-it data was easier than having to hear (and later see) Hawkeye swoop over me and laugh. Maybe Sweety was right. This was his Brahmastra … creep! He laughed like that on purpose.

Aside: Sweety Chopra was my friend, confidante, gym, kick-boxing and Zumba partner, neighbour, partner-in-crime, all rolled into one. Till two months back, she had been my colleague at EOFA, the non-profit organisation, an NGO where I go to get tortured in the name of employment. However, better sense seemed to have prevailed and she quit EOFA after an eventful week when she decided that she had subjected herself to enough torture. Now she is having a blast, hitchhiking her way around Continental Europe with Divya Sehgal, a stuck-up bitch but close friend of Sweety's, who also quit her frustrating job in the same bloody week!

"*Theek hai*, Rahul. I will try to send you the data as soon as I can."

With my tail between my legs, exuding super dedication to my fuck-all job, I, Oindrilla Roy, started work on this horrible May morning. Did I mention I was a research analyst? My job involved scouring through reams and reams of data and making some sense of it. At least that is what the JD said. But what I do at EOFA is bugger-all. I was, of course, hired to do some *dhaansu*-sounding research work, on the field, working at the grassroots level. What I do instead, is some modification of a glorified executive assistant and designer. I schedule meetings for Rahul, prepare *his* presentations and help overpaid professionals (from one of the Big 4 consultancies) with *their* research work and make colourful reports using Canva. Fuck-all work and for that, imagine I have some fancy-schmancy master's degree!

As I squinted at the computer, trying to meet Hawkeye's unreasonable deadline, I heard Ma bellow my name from below. She was ordering me to come home early from office to feed the dogs. Ma had some important meeting with the

Joint Secretary this afternoon, making it impossible for her to come back home to feed her babies. Now who would tell Hawkeye about this new development? He would freak out, *pakka*. I will have to listen to some long fuck-it-all speech about how work comes first and how I should not let my commitment and dedication lag—it being my first job and all. So be it then. I cringed, ready for another dreadful day. Thankfully by God's grace, Baba came to my rescue. He offered to take over the afternoon dog-feeding duties for the day. Such a relief. Phew!

2

A few hours later

Deadline met, data submitted, e-mails answered, matters solved and feeling rather pleased with myself, I reached office that morning around 11 a.m. The fact that Hawkeye was away for that meeting made office much more appealing. But one must give it to the EOFA top management, dude. To whatever extent possible, they did ensure that the employees didn't mind coming to work.

Situated in a swanky building in the uber-cool Cyber City locality in Gurugram, the EOFA office offered all amenities that one could think of. Free coffee, snacks, gym, spa—you name it, and they have it. Something unheard of in our sector. EOFA, by the way, stands for Equal Opportunity For All. It worked to uplift the downtrodden, poor and all other folk who had no employment opportunities. It was another matter that I was yet to figure out how EOFA did that. Anyway, the poor employee got sucked in, seeing all the jazz, and didn't even realise that essentially EOFA was a piece of shit!

After two days of no maid at home and no breakfast and other domestic tortures, the plush tenth floor office felt like absolute bliss. I found myself singing as I breathed in the mildly perfumed scented air outside the elevator. It did feel good to come to work.

"Look look, Oindrilla has replied to the mail in the morning. We need to show her, her place."

I stopped singing.

It was that new Comms lady (*high pitched, shrieking aunty, complete bitch*), talking to the old Comms lady (who seemed like a lost, gentle soul with no passion but also one complete bitch). Especially, ever since the new one joined, the Communications team at EOFA had been strutting around the office, throwing their combined weight (*which is quite a bit*) around. All these two elderly aunties did was make a few calls, yell at a few vendors and look important. Not surprising that Hawkeye got along fairly well with both bitch aunties, old and new. *If all they have to do is bitch, they can do it softly, no?!* The whole office and its uncle could listen to the new bitch aunty (NBA). The old bitch aunty (OBA) was chuckling and doing *haan-mein-haan.*

I entered softly. Those aunties, lost in their own cackle, did not notice my entry. *Waise bhi*, there was a lot of mess going on in the office since morning. Zarine, our sweet, funny receptionist was yelling at one of the office boys. Something was wrong with her morning cup of coffee.

EOFA began to awaken and come alive only by 11 a.m. All my friends, including Zarine showed up by 10:30 a.m. Hawkeye, the HR team, the admin guys and the bitch aunties come by 9:30 a.m., probably to impress the management, *ki saara kaam* only these people did and rest were *wellas* and *nikammas*.

Though I think the truth is they have no lives. Hawkeye is forever replying to e-mails—no matter which hour of the day. Yes, mysteriously once in a while, he mentions his poor family—wife and two daughters. They get used as some excuse. Daughter no. 1 is not well; daughter no. 2 has school orientation ... so on and so forth. Now the bitch aunties supposedly are married (not to each other as of now), but seeing how they chuckle and giggle, soon they should just!

As you can make out, I couldn't stand the Comms team.

I drew in a deep breath and walked towards my corner-side cubicle, a much-coveted bright spot overlooking the jazzy Cyber Hub.

"Oindrilla ... you are here. Finally! Did you hear about the Shillong fiasco?" That was Tejas Sharma, project manager, teammate and most importantly, my office buddy. Tejas was forever keyed in to all the office gossip. Maybe it was because he was so nice—genuinely so. He was pally with each of the 100–150 employees of EOFA, including the office boys. Admirable, I think. I would love to be like that but there was a hitch—one has to like people. I do not like people. I know I am not much liked either. Not that I mind at all. But Tejas, I liked. Very much!

"*Na baba*, no clue. What happened in Shillong? Wasn't that where that Vinay-Shinay fellow was posted to last month?

Aside: Vinay was a dumbass, high-flying consultant—one whose research work I landed up doing, most of the time, while he made the big bucks on account of being employed with one of the Big 4. As in this sector, like elsewhere, I would think, the Big 4 get pulled into all these great transformational projects. Contract bagged, some know-it-all consultants get sent to lord it over us. Of the two consultants I closely interacted with, this Vinay character had been the irritating one. Sraboni, the other one, was a sweet, hardworking gentle girl. Also helps that she was a country cousin and she could not stand Vinay either.

What had Vinay gone and done? Whatever it was, served the bloody bugger right!

Tejas, always happy to get his share of attention, took his time as he settled down quite comfortably, grabbing a packet of popcorn that was on my desk.

"Hey that is mine." *I am a popcorn addict – minimum three packets a day. No one, and I repeat, no one gets to touch my popcorn.*

"Gossip *sunna hai ki nahin?*"

"Ok fine," my love for gossip about despicable Vinay was stronger than popcorn love at that moment. I shut up and watched my popcorn disappear, much to my chagrin.

"So, our dear Vinay is in trouble. He goes to Shillong, behaves like some mini *laat saab* and has rubbed all the field functionaries the wrong way. They went and complained to the Deputy Commissioner who called our MD *(hereby known as Big Boss)* with one message—this bugger had to leave; else EOFA could say goodbye to the project. And so it has been. Vinay was given the marching orders, not only from Shillong but also from EOFA. His great office can post him with whomsoever they please."

"Ooh, this sure is good stuff. Solid solid *khabar.*" I squealed in sheer excitement, dropping my expensive phone in the process and eliciting some scornful looks. From the bitch aunties, of course!

Did I mention that the bitch aunties had their cubicles close to mine? This was a bit of an issue. The two landed up eavesdropping on most of my gossip sessions, while they themselves were clever enough to conduct their own sessions elsewhere. Bah! Like I gave a damn. And this was too good a news right in the morning. I smiled icily at the staring bitch aunties and continued squealing to Tejas. "This DC fellow is too good, man! He has sussed out that Vinay fuckwit in no time, and has done what Hawkeye and our great management couldn't do. He has some balls. I like him!"

"I hope you care to remember that this is an office and not your college hangout. You both are disturbing the rest of us," chimed the old bitch aunty in her most supercilious tone. The new one rolled her eyes and did not even attempt to hide that smile. *Argh, these two women!*

Poor Tejas was chastened and hurriedly went back to his cubicle, apologising for any inconvenience. *Inconvenience, my ass!*

The old biddies had been definitely hanging on to each and every word of his with bated breath. It was only when they had heard what they wanted to hear that their drama started.

I focussed on some shitty stuff that had been pending for a while, fairly content with my state. No Hawkeye yet and I was well-fed and rested. However, my general state of contentment and peace with the world was not to last long. Shortly after this conversation, Hawkeye made his annoying presence felt again.

"Oindrilla, we need to talk. Now."

One look at his constipated face, and I knew his fuck-all meeting hadn't gone well. The whys and whats of which would soon be told to me in great detail. I got a couple of minutes' reprieve. Hawkeye was smiling his 'pleasantest' smile at the old bitch aunty and making conversation. Of course, his interest was reciprocated. Usually, the new bitch aunty was the one who batted her eyelids more and listened in rapt attention when the constipated Hawkeye expounded his *tatti* theories about the world. But that lady in question was not there at the moment. She was probably tormenting the two *baccha* graphic designers. I stood up, trying to urge Hawkeye towards the meeting room. But *usko hint lena ho tab na.* Old bitch aunty was laughing huskily and telling him all about her daughter's annual day. Hawkeye was mesmerised and started recounting some anecdote about his daughter's annual day function. *Abe in buddhon ke paas kuch aur nahin hai kya batiyane ko?*

I shuffled my feet and dropped my pen. But to no avail. As I stood fidgeting, preparing for my verbal execution, the new bitch aunty made her appearance.

"Rahul, *aap aa gaye? Kaise hain?*"

Wah wah, so much attention! Constipated Hawkeye was virtually beaming! *Should I be happy? If he is that happy, then there is a possibility of me being spared.*

After an agonizing 5-10 minutes, this *buddhe-logon ka* camaraderie and *pyaar* got over and we proceeded towards the meeting room. While Hawkeye looked important and all, I followed him like a meek mouse. *Okay, that could be an exaggeration. No one can call me meek, though.*

I found out that all the morning's data analysis was a big waste as the potential client wanted something else altogether. Moreover, during the meeting, Hawkeye discovered two errors in the goddamn analysis and then he got that call about the Shillong fiasco. Please note, the great consultancy firm upon which we shower much moolah is particularly useless. Usually, all the error finding in data is done by poor me and when the data is cleaned up, the useless consultants get the accolades. Today, however, in my hassled state, I seemed to have let these pass. *Ufff.* Hawkeye took out all *bhadaas* of the failed meeting upon poor *moi*. I sat there, looking adequately contrite with downcast eyes and all.

When I was finally allowed to have a say, I patiently explained that the data we received was absolute shit.

Hawkeye surprisingly agreed with me and in a rare moment of confession, admitted that these blue-eyed boys and girls were such a burden on EOFA and totally not required. I was zapped. For the first time I looked at the constipated Hawkeye in a sudden new light. Here, all this while I had thought that he was the one who got them onboard the project. Then I found out that he had no clue as to why they were there either. I prodded, gently of course. Why were they there? Who in our senior management wanted them in? But Hawkeye was way too clever for my liking and did not let me in on this bit of office gossip. He changed the topic and I made a mental note to find out more about this from Tejas. But that was for later. As of now, I had to pay attention, rapt attention to the line of questioning I was being subjected to. No scope of day dreaming, as I hated being shouted at, and Hawkeye was one impatient guy.

Beep. Beep.

My mobile. I had forgotten to put it on silent. I ignored the message. Two minutes later, it started ringing. I tried ignoring it and kept nodding my head to whatever it was that Hawkeye was going on and on about. But the caller was equally persistent, if not more.

Five minutes into this silent war of resistance between the caller and me, Hawkeye gave up and said, "Oindrilla, your phone."

I looked at the phone. It was Ma.

"Tinku, where are you? You have to get home now!"

"What happened?" I panicked and conjured (thank my wild imagination) that something had happened to my father or my grandparents or my Boston-based uncle (whom I am extremely close to).

"I cannot get back home. Baba also can't. An urgent meeting has come up or so he says. Who will feed the dogs? Go home now and feed the dogs."

"Oh, I will check with my boss."

"Ok. Tell him that this is an emergency and leave now," my mother commanded before she slammed the phone down.

Oh God, fuck my life. I looked at Hawkeye sheepishly, who by now had guessed that something was up. He probably heard Ma clearly (she was always loud) or perhaps had gathered that all was not well, thanks to the dying duck expression on my face.

"*Jaana hai*? Problem *hai*? *Theek hai*."

I gawped, nodded and added, "Hmm, I will be back as soon as I can."

What an idiot I am. Why did I have to blurt that out? Could I not have just asked for half a day's leave?

But the damage had already been done. Hawkeye nodded and said, "Ok." So there, now I had to dash from Gurgaon to Vasant Kunj in flat 25 minutes, feed the dogs and then hurry back to this place. What the hell!

***

I booked an Ola and then tried seeing the best in this situation. The phone buzzed again. It was Sweety. She wanted to meet up for drinks later that evening. That pissed me off further. No way would Hawkeye allow me to leave early that evening. What if she came here and we met at Cyber Hub instead? Hmm … I messaged back. She replied almost instantly. She and Divya would be here around 7:30 p.m. *Abey* … why should I have to *jhelo* Divya? I wanted to meet Sweety. *Baba re*, I had a long day and a long evening ahead.

Forget the evening, the rest of the day turned out to be *maha* eventful too. When I got back to the office post my jig from Cybercity Gurgaon to Vasant Kunj, a huge surprise (or not) awaited me. It so happened that there was a management team meeting that was called urgently to come up with a master plan to combat the ongoing Shillong crisis.

Needless to say, my nemesis (Hawkeye and his two friends, the bitches) attended it and one of the bitch aunties volunteered my services (because 'Oindrilla is so efficient and so hardworking'; 'Since she is a Bong, she would also be able to gel in that part of the country, no? Food and language would hardly be a problem') to go and help sort the mess out. The old fogies in senior management lapped it up. You see, I might have cribbed and complained but, make no mistake, I had always been a bloody professional at work. So, the management team, in general, loved me. I was an asset to the organisation, if I may say so!

I came back to find out from Tejas (whose narration was saturated with much drama and action) that I was being packed off to Shillong, for three months. *Three months? Shillong? The bitch aunties had indeed royally screwed me.* I breathed in and breathed out. I calmed myself down, and did not have an outburst, much to the surprise of Tejas, who was preparing me for Hawkeye's formal intimation of the management's decision.

If I had taken Tejas' announcement so calmly, I was calmness personified when Hawkeye formally told me. (I kept smiling, with so much fortitude that the bitch aunties were shocked. Both the ladies had been watching me with unabashed glee, waiting for me to flinch or protest or crib or just abuse someone.)

Truth be told, I liked field trips. They gave me a chance to get out of the stuffy atmosphere at work and see the real world out there. A welcome break from my largely cocooned upper middle-class existence. So as a rule, in general, field trips were welcome. Until now, that is.

Reason – I had just come back from a rather longish stint in a small village in the central part of the country. After having spent six months in a district controlled by the Naxalites, with no electricity, nor the Internet and frequent kidnappings and other violent attacks, it had been my humble request to my *wonderful* manager that I not be sent to such a place for at least three months. And this was why the bitch aunties were so gleeful. They had successfully ensured that the management ignored my humble request. However, the calmer I remained, without using any cuss words (mentally even), and smiled, it struck me that a field trip to Shillong was in fact akin to a holiday! It would be a welcome reprieve from the household chores, thanks to my family's track record in retaining help. Wow, keeping quiet and not yelling or cursing and instead thinking over a matter actually worked! How come I had not realised this earlier? Despite Ma and Baba telling me always to think first and react later! *Thank you bitch aunties*. Ma and Baba would be so proud of me.

It was thus settled. Hawkeye told me that he would speak with the local team and the district administration to get the logistics and other arrangements sorted out.

Shillong it was to be, the following Monday.

3

"What? Shillong? Why? When? Did you not just come back from Raipur or Raigarh or some such place? *Arre* you know what I mean."

Later that evening, I was sitting in one of those yellow-orange chairs in the lovely parasol-shaded terrace at this happening bar at Cyber Hub; the one that I could peek into from my tenth floor office. Sweety and that Divya woman were seated opposite me and Sweety was the one hurling all these questions. I was about to reply to this barrage when I got diverted by a lot of ruckus at the table across us. I was probably spacing out and enjoying the moment by just being there.

Some aunty was celebrating her birthday and many other aunties were cheering rather loudly. Gurgaon (or make that South Delhi) aunties were a breed in themselves. One would think, at least I naively did, that people mature with age and start behaving so. But not with this breed. The older they got the sillier they behave and act. For one, they all wear clothes—latest brand, style and all—irrespective of whether they fit or not. Now, the lady in front of us was apparently celebrating her forty-fifth, a milestone in itself, I get that. But what I did not understand (and I think neither did Sweety and even Divya for that matter) was that why she had stuffed herself into this teeny-weeny dress that had her curves (flabby, if I may say so) spilling out of everywhere. As if the bling wasn't already offensive enough to the eyes of those around.

Well, enough of bitchiness from me. Why, snooty Divya was rubbing off on me by just sitting next to me. Wow! As I ruminated upon the Divya effect, she uttered some magnificently bitchy words that were worthy of her name! Divya Sehgal, born into old money and riches and brought up as only a spoilt Delhi-ite could be, was gawping at the ongoing ruckus. In a tone dripping with scorn, Divya then went on to postulate her views on the nouveau riche of Gurgaon. Quite clearly, these nouveau-riche aunties of Gurgaon did not live upto her sophisticated South Delhi standards. Sweety was looking at Divya with such *louvv* that I felt like shaking her violently. Let me make it clear. I couldn't stand Divya Sehgal. Or for that matter most people I met. For but the love of gawddd, I could not fathom what Sweety saw in her.

Sweety and I go back to the time when I had just moved to Delhi from Kolkata. This was right after school when I had completely screwed up in my Class 12 board exam. Reeling with a disastrous result and a broken heart (but that's not really important now), and not wanting to stay with grandparents any longer, I had flown to Delhi on an absolute whim to appear for an entrance exam, to study Korean at a South Delhi university. Why Korean, you may ask? Actually, the application form had been filled up in a drunken stupor, on the day of my Maths exam, when I was sure I would flunk. As I howled and tanked up in my room at my grandparents' place in Kolkata, my cousin Ankita asked me innocently what I would do, now that flunking my board examinations seemed like a strong possibility. Barring studying an obscure language, was there anything I could do, I wondered loudly as I continued to howl. That girl immediately googled and found out about this course and before I knew it, I had applied for the entrance exam. That was how I had studied this course (despite actually not flunking Grade 12) and ultimately ended up in EOFA!

Ma and Baba back then had been posted in two different parts of the country. When they heard I had run away (leaving a note behind and all) to study Korean, they naturally freaked out. Ma was ready to land in Delhi and drag her deranged daughter away. Baba was less concerned because he was certain the deranged daughter would not get admission and would be back in Cal in no time. Baba's assurance and Ma's vile boss ensured that the daughter was spared the dragging. However, to everyone's shock (including mine), I got admission to this course, despite getting a fairly disastrous score in the entrance exam. The real reason for my making it to the Korean language programme at this great university was that there were a mere five applications apropos to the expected class strength of 60 that year.

Why KOREAN? Why at a university in Delhi? No fucking clue. What was I thinking anyway? As I mentioned earlier, I act first and think later. During that phase, I had stopped thinking. I was upset and heartbroken. And was looking for a quiet, unobtrusive existence in some corner of the hostel at this university. That too in a city I certainly did not like at first sight but where I could fade into oblivion.

Around this time, Ma and Baba both landed up in Delhi on deputations. (Now that I think about it, this whole move was rather timely) They definitely would have pulled some strings with the higher-ups to move to Delhi, in order to keep an eye on their deranged daughter for sure! Which explains the VK rental flat as well.

The crux of this ramble is that I ended up in a room in my parents' second-floor flat in Vasant Kunj, a popular middle-class locality in South West Delhi. Fading into an alcohol-induced oblivion in a hostel room was to remain a distant dream at that juncture! Incidentally, we still lived in Vasant Kunj but not in the same second-floor flat.

Coming back to the move to VK that summer, the Roy family moved in together shortly before my classes at the university were to commence. Ma and Baba were excited, as usual. My mother, please note, was always in a state of hyperventilation. Baba is the calm one, usually wall-like, in his disposition; not at all prone to mood swings, which we Roy women were known for. That summer, Baba also looked excited. Or was he agitated? Poor man, now that I think about it, I caused them enough anguish with my knee-jerk actions.

***

It was shortly after our move to Vasant Kunj that I had met Sweety.

Funnily I still remember the day we met, rather clearly. Now VK flats were typical DDA flats—small, crumbling and cramped. The walls were so thin that you could very well hear what went on in the next house! I was unable to sleep the first few days. I would toss and turn and try to sleep with a pillow on my head, just to drown out the noises from outside—stray dogs barking, the mad old lady from the flat opposite raving and ranting every night about being abandoned, and then the newly-wed grunting on the first floor! Every bloody night—it was the same story. I was already a heartbroken zombie, and soon I became a sleepless, heartbroken zombie. I overheard Ma and Baba also discussing the various noises. Ma was agitated and Baba was reassuring her that we would get adjusted to this new place. Typical Baba reaction—he firmly believed that things would fall into place eventually. And they did. We got used to the noises at night, learned to fall asleep and made friends. Coming back to the day I met Sweety, I remember it was at the bus-stop. It was my first day at the university—a typical slushy, muggy Delhi monsoon morning. Everything was dusty and icky around me. As I stood, waving my umbrella (to shoo away the mosquitoes), she walked towards me, looking bright and chirpy, clad in a fuchsia shirt and cropped jeans. She was doing the same, shooing mosquitos, albeit with a dainty hand fan. Sweety is very pretty, in a wholesome Punjabi way. Given her tall, statuesque figure, smooth, shiny hair and a classic oval face with big eyes, she does not fail to turn heads, no matter where she goes. Seven years ago, as a gawky eighteen-year-old, when most of us looked plain weird, she had those eye-catching looks. Looks that made even a complete surly zombie like me notice her. *Is she the girl Ma told me about? The one in the ground-floor flat, whom Ma wanted me to befriend?* Well, soon the bus that would take me to the university arrived, filled to the brim, with people spilling over. As I was debating whether to get in or not, I found myself not only jostled and pushed right into it but also pinched in the butt! What the bloody fuck! Using my umbrella as a weapon, I thrust it right at the molester, jabbing the bastard where it hurt the most and created a huge ruckus. Sweety, a witness to the incident, jumped right into the fray and the man was shunted out of the bus. By the time we got down near the university, a camaraderie had been forged.

Sweety and I were indeed neighbours (yes, she was the girl in the ground floor flat that Ma had been telling me about). I found out that Sweety was a first-year student of Applied Psychology in a prestigious girls' college in South Delhi, which was nowhere near my university. However, the guy she was crazy about those days studied in my university. So, for a major part of the next two years (as long as she was with him), she would come with me. That was also the last time I took a bus in this city – fucking molesting creatures, those.

Over the next few months, I recovered, much to my own surprise. My college years flew by. At the end of three years, I had learnt (somewhat) a brand new language that I had no bloody interest in and made many friends at the university. Sweety and I were best friends, spending each and every moment possible together, when not in college. Nights were passed in drunken stupor, in either my room or hers. I am certain Ma and Baba knew but I think they were relieved that I was past my Cal heartbreak. We took up hobbies, partied, went to the parlour, travelled on holidays to nearby locales, and basically lived in each other's homes. Oh yes, there were the occasional boyfriends, who would come and go, but we took notes upon whom not to date and whom to try to hook up with. Life was good so far!

We even made plans for our postgraduate degree together. After three years of learning a language that was to be of no bloody use, I decided to go the MBA route just like each one of my friends. Sweety and I studied together (sessions that had more to do with giggling, bitching and drinking than actual *padhai*), and inspite of that finally we made it! To our great joy and happiness, we both got admitted to the same B-school, a fairly prestigious one, and so our next phase as hostel roomies in a city far from Delhi thus commenced. It was during this B-school stint that Madam Divya Sehgal came into our lives. We met during the orientation week in the loud, noisy mess. Divya was in the same queue, like the rest of us, waiting to be served. Everyone has heard of love at first sight. With this bitch Divya, for me, it was a case of HATE at first sight. The rest of the long, meandering queue waited patiently for the old bearer who doled out *khana* and served plate by plate. Not Miss Hoity-Toity. She whined in her nasal voice, and then was downright rude to the old bearer. This got my goat. Who the fuck did this entitled bitch think she was! Not one to shut up, I intervened and stood up for this *bechara* apologetic, old bearer and told the fucking chick to wait. Divya, probably never having been confronted, kept quiet but sulked throughout dinner, shooting me hate-filled glances. Her behaviour elsewhere on campus, wasn't endearing either. She whined and wheedled, using her charms to get her way. Oh yes, she was attractive in a dusky, earthy way. Make no mistake, it was not her looks that bothered me. My best friend was prettier than her. It was the shameless and manipulative way in which she used those charms to have her way that pissed me off. This, coupled with that entitled stance (much more than my own entitled attitudes) was enough to make me dislike her. The next week, she and Sweety teamed up in the same group for a class assignment where they hit it off and how.

4

"You know, Oinks, Divya is really nice. You will like her when you get to know her."

"*Kya ghanta* nice! With her nose high up in the air, how on earth do you find her nice, Sweets?"

But Sweety being Sweety took it upon herself to get us to know one another. A painful meeting that! My redeeming feature (in her eyes) was the fact that my parents were bureaucrats! In my eyes, she had no such feature. An out and out South Delhi snob from Greater Kailash, she was too arrogant and privileged. I made no bones about disliking the dame. She couldn't stand my sight either. But our common love for Sweety ensured that we tolerated each other and an uneasy acquaintance ensued. We would meet and be civil, but this was always at Sweety's behest. She and Divya would spend hours and hours together while I made new friends. And I did not mind. My day-to-day life was rather hectic. Besides the gruelling coursework, my social life was frenzied. Too much socialising was the order of the day—I had class friends, library friends, yoga and kickboxing friends, and finally dancing and drinking buddies. Since school-time heartbreak was long past and I had mostly recovered, I also had a couple of flings—no serious relationships, just sex! The MBA course, in general, was great fun. During campus placements, Sweety and I both got picked by EOFA. I had gotten an offer from a big IT consultancy firm in Bengaluru as well, but being the completely directionless moron that I was, I chose the NGO EOFA. Reason – its office was in Gurgaon and I could live with my folks and Sweety would also be there! Somewhere in my moronic mind also lurked a fucking idealistic idiot who thought that much good could come from using the learned skills to benefit the underprivileged.

Divya got placed in Delhi too – with a pseudo-intellectual outfit dedicated to saving and protecting Indian art and architecture funded by a big IT house. Definitely the place after Divya's own arty-farty pseudo heart! Sweety also tried to see if there were any vacancies there. By the end of our MBA, Divya and Sweety were literally stuck to each other. Where one went, the other followed. There were many leery jokes about their sexual orientation and honestly, even I speculated, at times, that they were seeing each other. But I couldn't care less whether Sweety was a lesbian or bisexual. She was a generous, reliable friend and I loved her. Whether she was doing Divya or not, it was none of my fucking business.

And so it was that we came back to Delhi and began a new phase. It helped tremendously to have Sweety with me during my initial days at EOFA. If the B-school experience was great fun, and had me raring to go, EOFA was like a cold shower of reality poured straight onto my nerves.

Coming back to the present day, rather evening, Sweety and Divya were excitedly filling me in on the details of their backpacking trip across Europe. I was zoning out despite trying to focus. No, I would have loved to listen to Sweety and her tales, but it was the nasal voice of Divya darling that was pissing me off. Soon there was respite. Sweety again pestered me about Shillong. I reluctantly told her all that had passed. Just when it looked like our conversation was over, Sweety, looking solemn, held my hand and said, "Oinks, we need your help."

"Huh, sure, what happened, Sweets?"

Looking a bit sheepish, she looked at Divya and started, "Actually, sorry I haven't spoken about this to you before. But I need to tell you now. I ... well we are in love."

"Who? What? You are in love with that Akshay? Seriously? Since when?"

Akshay was the poor sod whom Sweety had been stringing along since the past two years. She called him her on-and-off boyfriend. Poor fucking sod. First, he got dumped by Divya and then he found Sweety or rather Sweety found him! But why?

Sweety and Divya both were looking at me as if I had gone mad. "*Arre*, no! Not Akshay. Divya and I are in love. We want to be together forever."

Now it was my turn to gawk at them. Sweety and Divya? Eww... Aargh no... Now, please don't get me wrong, I most certainly do not suffer from any degree of homophobia, and I certainly had speculated, a teeny-weeny bit, back in the B-school days about them! Sweety or anyone for that matter could be anything ranging from hetero to pan to homo to demi or any which sexual. It was her choice of partner that was making me cringe. Why Divya? Why she of all the people? But I guess, it was fucking expected. Both Sweety and I were idiotic when it came to our choice of partners. Pathetic taste and complete lack of any sane judgment really. Bravo!

"Oinks, stop gawping. Since when have you become so judgmental?"

"Oops, sorry, no … erm, not really. I am only surprised. No, no, I am happy for you guys," I countered, trying to sound my cheeriest best.

Sweety rolled her eyes. "Stop, Oinks. Don't fake it. You suck at this. *Muuh band kar.* I felt guilty about not sharing this with you."

"Sorry, sorry, this did take me by surprise. But I really am happy for you." To cover my complete shock at my best friend coming out, and to not make her feel miserable, I jumped up and gave them both a big bear hug.

Divya smiled, a bit superciliously, or maybe that was what I felt, "Glad that you are okay with it, Oindrilla. Sweety was worried about how you would take it."

How would I take it? Well, I am in shock. No no, not because my best friend has come out; but because she is sharing such an important piece of information, in front of Divya, whom I do not like and who now is the love of Sweety's life! OMFG!!

"I told you, darling. Oinks always means well," Sweety replied, beaming.

I smiled again and this time, with as much sincerity as I could inject into my voice, I replied, "I won't deny I am a bit zapped but please I am happy for you both and will always wish the best for you both. And now … that I am looking at you in a new light, you both err look cute together."

Luckily for me, precisely at that very moment, my phone rang. It was Ma. *Shit.* It was already 9:45 p.m. My parents, while modern in most respects, turned into ogres from the stone ages when it came to my schedule. No matter what, I had to be back home by 10 p.m. I know, it was fucking insane!

While all my friends had sleepovers during school time, I was the only kid not allowed to go for a sleepover. *Sigh*. Growing up was traumatic, man. But at that moment, my mom's yelling sounded like pure music. I could get away and digest the shock of Sweety and Divya being in love. I mumbled to Ma over the phone, looked apologetic, threw in my share of cash on the table and hurriedly left. *Phew*. What a fucking day it had been.

As expected, I was treated to an earful from Ma when I got home. Both she and Baba had been jittery, well they always were, unless and until I called them a hundred times to assure them that I was alright. The pains of being an only child, really. When I mentioned that I had been with Sweety, their shouting stopped. You see, they were very fond of Sweety. They saw her as the girl who managed to *thoko* some sense into their idiot daughter's head, when she needed it the most. Actually, it was true. She did. Oh Sweety, why Divya? If you had to pick a girlfriend, why not that sweet Pavitra, the one who used to work with us at EOFA? She was definitely more interesting and to top it all she only had eyes for Sweets. Well, guess I had to now come to terms with this icky-shicky development.

Over a cup of hot milk (which had to be taken mandatorily) before bed time, when Ma was watching one of those godawful shows on the telly and Baba was dozing next to her, I finally told them about the impending Shillong move.

"*Arre, eta ki*. Who will take care of the dogs?" was my mother's first reaction. Seriously man, her only daughter was leaving home and all she was bothered about were the fucking *kuttas*! And seeing her getting so perturbed about the *kuttas* and the fact that there was no sign of a maid, cook or driver, I was now relieved and thankful that I could run away from this mad house for a while. Baba was thankfully a bit more concerned; he wanted to know all the deets, how many months, why, where, etc., all of which I duly provided.

As we were discussing things that needed to be done before I moved the coming Monday, my mother got a crazy (*according to Baba*) idea. Please note, I had got all my impulsiveness and stubbornness from Ma. It suddenly struck her that she hadn't met her folks in a while. And so, it was decided. We would all go to Cal and meet the entire family and then Ma and Baba would drop me at Shillong by Sunday evening and get back to Delhi. (*Hein,* she had forgotten about her darling *kuttas* already?) Of course, her suggestion was much to my liking too. I had not met my cousin Ankita in ages and this would be a much-needed welcome break, especially in the light of recent developments.

My father bravely voiced the question that was going on in my head: what would we do with the dogs for three days? The answer was duly provided. Baba would stay back. Ma would accompany me. As Ma excitedly started preparing for our trip, surfing for tickets, and finalising travel plans, Baba announced that since it was close to midnight, he would retire for the day. As he walked out of the room, he smiled and winked at me. It was then that I realised, he never wished to come to Cal/Shillong at all. Very smartly, instead of crossing paths with Ma, he had led her to believe that it was her idea. *What a family! Fuck!*

5

Mornings were always full of drama in our household. When the maids were not there to create some ruckus and the dogs were quiet *bacchas*, Baba and Ma would step in to create some *hulla*. The next morning, it was all about Ma's excitement. She got some cheap last-minute deal on the tickets and was conveying her excitement in loud decibel levels, which woke me up. When I went down for breakfast, Ma told me that we were leaving that very evening and I was to take Thursday and Friday off. I was ordered to get to the airport in time, directly from office. Fuck. I had not applied for leave yet. Please note, at heart I was still a school girl who was afraid to tell the boss that I needed two days off. And worse, EOFA was like a school and Hawkeye, a horrid class teacher.

Looking at my dying duck expression, Ma bellowed some more. Usual lecture – that I was no longer in school and besides taking leave was my right as a dutiful employee and that every organisation had to honour and take care of its employees. As usual it ended with, "Do you want me to come and speak to your boss?" Oh no, no, definitely not. That clinched it.

I packed my *boriya* and *bistar* for roughly two weeks (work wear, home wear, going-out wear. Wait. Where would I go out in that fucking sleepy Shillong?) Since one never knows whom one may meet, one nice dress was kept handy.

Despite getting *gaalis* from mom about anything and everything – mornings were meant for mom to shout at us – by the time I left for office, I was in a good mood. Cal first, Shillong later, happy times are here, I thought! (Oh maybe they would be deferred for a bit.)

"Hello, Oindrilla! *Aaj toh* time *pe ho, he he he. Arre, kahan jaa rahi ho*? All this luggage?"

Fuck. Hawkeye is next to me as we wait for the elevator. Smile Oinks, don't gape.

"Hi, Rahul. *Main roz isi* time *pe aati hoon. Aap* late *kaise ho gaye aaj*?"

Idiot. Of all the things to blurt.

"*He he he*, your sense of humour is good. The traffic was bad today. *Waise toh* I leave home on time; after dropping my daughters ... *aaj toh* ..." *Yadda yadda yadda. Thank God, the man has gone off on a tangent! He loves the sound of his own nasal voice. Let him continue. Plaster that fake smile on your face now, Oinks.*

"... *Waise* you didn't answer my question yet?"

"What?" I was lost and had no clue what Hawkeye wanted to know. Luckily the elevator door opened and came to my rescue. Oh yes, my bags. Placing my bags into the elevator, I smiled (my sweetest best) and replied, "Ah Rahul, the bags? Planned to speak to you later in the day. Good that we met here. I need a leave."

"Leave. *Arre* Oindrilla, *aise kaise*? We have so much work. Don't you know that there is a meeting at the Ministry next week?"

Abe. Make your effing presentation yourself. Next week I will be in Shillong. Oh no. Will I have to make presentations for Rahul, while in Shillong? The reality of my fuck-all existence struck. Was that not what I did on my last outstation trip? NO NO NO...Control, babes, control.

"Sorry, I know this is rather sudden. Came up last evening. Need to stop by in Cal to visit Didama and Mamu-Mami before reporting at Shillong. My mom personally wanted to speak to you today about it."

"*Oh uski kya zaroorat*? I understand. No problem. We can talk about the presentation later. No worries," said Rahul hurriedly as we stepped out of the elevator on the sixth floor.

Oindrilla Roy – you are a genius. That was an absolute masterstroke. Why had this not struck you earlier? Using Ma's name? It had to strike gold. Obviously OK, the thing was that Hawkeye was enamoured by and had a deep and abiding reverence for anyone who had cracked the civil services exam. Ma and Baba, as senior civil servants, naturally were high on the list of people to be revered. I suspected it had to do with the fact that he probably never got through – hence this fascination (he he).

Phew, now that the deed had been done and Rahul had been belled, I hoped that the rest of the day would pass in a jiffy. It did, barring one teeny-weeny episode that had been playing on my mind since it occurred. All thanks to the two bitch aunties. They just couldn't leave me in peace, could they!

***

Tejas and I were heading back from lunch. I had overeaten as usual – which meant Tejas was forced to climb the stairs back. Huffing and puffing (that was me and not the super-fit Tejas), when we were about to open the rear door to the office – where the pantry was located – we overheard a (private) conversation. I stopped Tejas and signalled him not to speak a word. *Please note that being an anti-social person, I avoided everyone most of the time.* Tejas shook his head in that resigned way. Did I tell you about Tejas? Poor guy, this resigned expression was forever etched on his face. At the office, he had to manage me and at home, there was his fundoo, but yes, *thodi-si-pagal* wife, Suman! But that is for another time!

Back to the pantry where…

The bitch aunties were catching up over a cup of tea, and making eyes at Hawkeye (who else). Oh yes, Vikram was standing next to them. He handled HR for EOFA and was a carpool mate (and also a friend) of Hawkeye's. He got along well with NBA from what I had observed. Wonder why! Because he really wasn't bad; in fact, he was nice. (*Could be a pain in the ass slightly at times but that we all were. Vikram, with all his annoying quirks, still would win a contest for being one of the nicer people in EOFA.*)

NBA: Raaahul, the meeting in Shillong is planned for Tuesday, right? *Aapne booking kara li*?

Hawkeye: Aparna, yes, the meeting's on Tuesday, as of now. We should reach there on Sunday. Zarine is checking the ticket prices and hotel rates. Boss *ke* approval *ke baad* she said she would book.

NBA: Ah good. Oindrilla is leaving today? Won't she be travelling with us then?

Hawkeye: Oh, she needed two days off.

OBA: Umm, ok. *Oh*, Rahul, *aap itne* kind *ho*! *Chhutti ke liye kabhi na nahin karte*.

God knows why, at this point, all the three old people started chuckling! Vikram was clearly occupied with something else. He was rather silent – and no he wasn't the quiet type at all.

I was rather aghast at this pathetic attempt. That is if this was an attempt to flirt – otherwise I honestly didn't understand what was funny in this conversation. Hawkeye, puffed and chuffed, at this 'compliment' (if you may call this so!), started pontificating on the virtues of being a kind boss (MY FOOT!).

Vikram: *Isme* kind *kya hai*? It is her right as an employee. You guys carry on. I need to check on something the Boss wants.

Yay! Vikram! Thank you! Muah muah.

Hawkeye: Vikram is right. Also, *dekho*, Suchitra, one has to be understanding. *Bechari ladki bahut kaam karti hai*. Hardworking, good kid!

NBA: Agreed. Rahul. She is indeed good at her work, professional and hard-working. Does a brilliant job. If only she were a little less grumpy!

Arre, haan Suchitra, you are done with the annual report, no? Rahul, why don't you take a look at it, before it goes to the Boss?

Hawkeye: Yes, send it to me. I will. Boss is in one of his moods today…

The conversation came to an end and the pantry was clear.

Fuck! What was that?? I froze in the stairways, my mouth wide open!

"Oinks, can we also move? *Ab toh* eavesdropping also over. *Chalo!*"

"Tejas, wait. The new bitch aunty had some kind words to say about me! Is she ok? Did she get hit on the head by any chance today?"

"Don't be mean, Oinks. I told you, Aparna is nice. Think about it – rationally and objectively... She may not be the bitch you have imagined her to be. Neither is Suchitra."

"This is just freaking unbelievable. Whatever. I need to stop gawking and get done with that darned report."

The daze didn't last long! Hawkeye ensured that. Anyway, done with the impending report (finally), I found myself on the way to the airport ... in a cab ... with a nosy cab driver and Ma hollering over the phone.

Cabbie: Aap ko daant pad rahi hai?

Me: Ji haan, aap please *thoda tez chalayenge?*

Cabbie: Mataji theek hi keh rahi hain. Aapko jaldi nikalna chahiye tha office *se.*

Me: (exasperated) Ji, thoda jaldi please.

Now I was really not that late. With some 1.5 hours to go, I made it to the airport ... only to find out that my hollering Ma was not even there! What the fuck! Why was she yelling then?

Me: Ma, where are you?

Ma: On my way. You just board ok. I got late!

Me: Arre, why were you yelling at me then?

Ma: Because I didn't want both of us to miss the flight!

How on earth was one even expected to reply to this? *Uff,* what a crazy family!

As it turned out, neither of us missed our flight and we successfully boarded the plane...

6

The flight to Kolkata was stormy – no, I am not talking about the air turbulence outside. I was pissed with Ma and didn't talk to her properly. She was pissed with me about *hazaar* things and kept *sunaoing* me throughout the journey, much to my mortification.

More so because there was a fairly dishy looking guy sitting next to Ma. Well, that's what he seemed to me from what I could see. You see, only his side profile was visible and that was dishy. Couldn't see more – he had his face stuck between the pages of some *mota-sa* book. (OK, I was not staring. I was just trying to make sure whether he understood the *gaalis* my mom was belting out. Oh shit, he had a smile on his face. He probably understood every single one of those! Must be a Bong guy – who else even goes to that sleepy city. Oh good lord, the mortification!)

Note to self – stop over-reacting and analysing AND STARING, you numbskull!

"*Maa, chhup koro*. You are disturbing everyone. Too loud." I whispered, hoping to *shaant karo* my Ma.

"Tinku, unacceptable – totally unacceptable this is. OK, I will stop."

Thank heavens. Ma stopped. To avoid any more embarrassments, I buried myself in my Kindle. Better to look preoccupied and busy. *Waise bhi* Ma had made my *izzat ka falooda* in front of a perhaps-dishy-stranger.

Anyways, flight over, destination reached. Ah Kolkata! Here I was – again – after all these years! Ever since my flight to Delhi years ago to nurse my broken heart, I had steadfastly avoided travelling to Cal. Luckily for me, Didama, Ankita, Mamu-Mami would drop by in Delhi regularly – I never felt the need either.

As the plane landed on the runway at Netaji Subhash Chandra Bose airport, I realised how much I missed the goddamn sleepy city. It was as if I had been punched in the gut. *Fuck. I love Cal and have missed it so very much.* Suddenly I felt tearful and emotional! Fuck! What was going on? My brain definitely was addled. *It must be PMS then. What was the date again?*

"Tinku, stop day-dreaming. Get up. Where did you put my suitcase?"

Trust Ma to kick me back to action. I snapped out of my reverie and saw that our fellow-passengers were behaving as expected. Jostling and pushing each other to pull out the luggage from the overhead compartments. *Pata nahin kahe ka hurry. Ab* when the whole world was racing to get their suitcase, how could Ma be behind? She was getting antsy, I knew. For once the antsiness was not thanks to me. The guy with the dishy side profile in our row, on the aisle seat, was still buried in his book.

Ma, whose patience (or the lack of it) was legendary (in our family, that is) had to butt in. "Excuse me, *beta*, could you kindly get up? We need to get going."

Poor guy – the might-be-dishy-guy had no choice but to take his face out of the book it was buried in. After all, he had come in contact with the crazy Roy ladies.

He smiled. First at Ma and then at me.

"Sure, Aunty, I will get up now. Hello Oindrilla, how are you? Do you remember me?"

OH BLOODY HELL! It was Vivek. Vivek Rao – the reason why I messed up my twelfth standard – the one and only true love of my inconsequential life so far.

"Stop gawping, and answer him, Tinku. Do you know him?" Ma nudged me as she turned on her charm on the bloody jerk.

"Hello, *beta*. Sorry I don't seem to place you. And neither does Oindrilla. Maybe, you can refresh her memory."

Aaargh, no, my memory did not need any refreshing. I had spent the past fucking odd number of years trying to forget Vivek Rao. What luck – total *phooti kismet* and all. First time back in Kolkata after donkey's years and who do I meet? Vivek Rao.

Breathe in. Calm. Breathe out. Get a grip.

"Hello, Vivek. I do remember you. Sorry, it took me a while to place you. How are you?"

HOW ON EARTH HAD I NOT RECOGNISED THAT SIDE PROFILE OF HIS? You see, in the bygone days, I had stared at him so much that I thought his face was imprinted in my mind, heart and soul. *Yuck. Oindrilla Roy, stop being pathetic*!

He smiled again – sending my stupid, idiotic, broken-into-a-thousand-pieces heart into yet another tizzy. I was almost about to smile back at him but better sense prevailed. Giving him a rather disinterested look, I started looking at my phone, pretending to be engrossed in a WhatsApp conversation. (That was basically an SOS being sent to Sweety and Ankita along with explicit instructions NOT to call immediately.) I clearly did not want to speak to this man. The people in the aisle started moving – Phew! Vivek stood up to pick up his luggage. I quickly used this opportunity to pick up my and Ma's hand bags as well, and to avoid any conversation. (Yes, I know, rude, grumpy and outright weird – I was. I held this person solely responsible for the shit I went through and the reason I studied Korean.)

"Can you please move ahead? Ma and I are in a bit of a hurry."

"Sure," he replied rather frostily, or so I thought, and felt strangely miserable. But that was before the cheeky jerk added (in a low voice – only for me to hear).

"*Aha* – you still don't want to speak with me! Trying to run away, huh? But why? Before you scoot away again, tell me, how have you been, Oinks?" Vivek whispered in my ears, in his low deep voice – melting my idiotic, pathetic heart into a puddle.

I pretended not to hear and continued looking into my phone, which rang that very moment. Hawkeye.

Oh, I love you, Hawkeye!

"Yes, Rahul."

"Oindrilla, sorry I know you are on *chhutti* – and you have probably just landed. *Woh* Ministry *ke liye jo* presentation *banayi thi na*, last week, can you resend it?"

My irritating boss – as usual – had missed my mail. Hawkeye had to always call back, years after a mail had been sent, to ask me to resend it to him. How unprofessional. The guy had some 1000s of unread mails – which he then used to show off to those bitch aunties, constantly trying to impress them as to how busy he was. Half those emails were probably spam mails from all that web surfing he did!

The only difference was that this time, I did not mind. AT ALL. Any distraction was welcome. Bring the work on! I was willing to resend every mail I had sent over the past one year. Anything to keep me staring at the phone.

The gods were kind. A WhatsApp message!

Sweety: Who? Vivek?? Ooooooh the man-whose-name-must-not-be-mentioned and hasn't been mentioned since the time we met?

O: Yes, yes that very man!

S: Aha, refresh my memory please. What is it that you abhor about him?

O: DIVYA, give Sweety her phone back!

S: Sorry sorry, didn't realise you would notice.

Not notice? As if I wouldn't know how my best friend sounded on chat. Well, whatever, considering I wanted a distraction – even Divya chatting with me as Sweety was fine.

Somehow, between Hawkeye texting and Divya chatting as Sweety, I managed to avoid Vivek completely and evade Ma's questioning, curious and somewhat murderous glances. (*I knew, I would be in for a massive interrogation on the way back home.*) After a few thwarted attempts at trying to talk to me (*or so I would like to think*), Vivek got busy – fetching his luggage, attending a couple of calls – and did not make any further friendly overtures.

FUCK, why then did I feel sad?

Because you are a pathetic loser, Oindrilla Roy. Dimaag naamak koi vastu hai hi nahin tumhare paas!

As Ma and I walked out of the airport, she got busy trying to spot Mamu. I felt tearful, miserable and utterly emotional. What a bloody homecoming this had been!

The ride back home was equally torturous. After hugging Mamu and Ankita and keeping the luggage in the boot, I sat in the car, and before Ma could ask a single question, I burst into copious tears.

Mamu and Ankita were flabbergasted.

"What happened to her? *Di*, did you both fight?"

"*Pishi*, is she happy or sad to see us?"

Ma, typically said – "*Arre* nothing. It is not you or me. Some *bechara* sweet-looking fellow. *Haan ... Bibek*, that was his name. It was him – was she happy or sad to see him, I don't know. It is all that fellow's doing."

"Vivek. Not *Bibek*, Ma!" (*Uff*, Idiot me! *Aise Meena Kumari moment mein bhi* nitpicking *ki aadat jaayegi nahin!*)

Ankita looked shocked. "Vivek. That Vivek? After all these years?"

I nodded, in between some more tears.

"*Bibek*, Vivek or whoever. Now stop crying. Every time you meet him or speak his name, you cry! You like him? Go tell him. You don't? Then tell him you don't! Why to cry? *Uff*. You girls!" Trust my own mother to pooh-pooh my *sadiyon ka* heartbreak in such a callous manner.

"Actually, *Pishi*, you are right. It is this simple. *Haan*, Tinku di, why are you crying? Did he do something? Say something mean? Misbehave?"

"*Hein*? Why would Vivek do something like that? If only he had. I could have whacked him and gotten this hurt and everything out of my system." I was flabbergasted at my cousin's airheaded remark.

Ma gave me one of her looks and started talking to Mamu. Once they ascertained that I was fine (for them if there was no bodily harm visible, one was fine), and that these tears were for some guy I saw on the plane, they lost interest in me and started talking to each other – excitedly. Rather it was Ma talking and Mamu listening.

With the elders engrossed in their conversation, Ankita came closer (we both were seated in the back) and whispered, "Tinku di, what happened? Are you okay?"

"I am okay – very okay. But I want to cry. Why the fuck did I have to meet him after all these years?" I sobbed harder.

"Oindrilla Roy, mind your language."

"Sorry, Ma. Bwahahwaa … but he did not even speak with me. How could he just walk away without even asking me how I was," I wailed some more.

"Tinku, YOU did not speak to him! YOU were the rude one. *Bechara,* he tried to make some kind of conversation. He did not just walk away. Stop howling now and blow your nose. This girl is getting more ridiculous by the day, Obir."

Well, this was a rather absurd conversation – come to think of it – I was howling to Ankita and Ma kept butting in. Mamu and Ankita both knew better than to say a word. The storm passed. By the time we reached home, I was done with my outburst and what followed was severe and terrible mortification. How pathetic could I be!

***

Finally, I started behaving more like an adult (and less deranged, as Ma put it) by the time we reached home. The next three days in Kolkata were plain blissful. Dida spoilt me silly; and so did Mamu-Mami. It had, after all, been a while since I had last visited them. Absolutely NO references were made to the-guy-who-must-not-be-named. I was lolling in bed with everyone serving me hand over feet – thank you Dida! Ma was her usual self – trying to get me off the bed but Dida intervened. It was pure bliss.

Friday evening, Saturday, and most of Sunday had been earmarked for Ankita. Despite not having lived in the same city for nearly a decade now, Ankita and I were extremely close. We always had been. Ma often wondered why!

I was/am cranky, rude and obstinate (Ma's astute words) and Ankita was/is sunshine, laughter, smiles, a bright ray of light! (How annoying) A complete *accha baccha* – she would not spill food (then or now) or make a mess, or throw a fit, or jump from here and there. Instead, she would preen and smile and be seated like a good porcelain doll. *You get the type, right?* Now, despite my inherent ill-tempered nature, I could not and would not be mean to my little sister. Oh, at times, of course I felt like pinching and punching her – but better sense had always stopped me from acting on my impulses. As we grew older, she acquired a lot of sense on top of the good girl halo. *Baap re* – even more annoying, wasn't it? But I loved her. Even though she was two years younger, she was the one I turned towards for advice – especially that year when I mucked up my Grade 12 exams (or so I thought I had)… She had been my anchor, my sister, my friend – Ankita!

Now however, when I think of it, if she were truly sensible, why on earth had she not stopped me from studying Korean? Who in their right minds studied Korean – of all the subjects. Maybe she wasn't that sensible after all!

What the fuck. I hadn't had such thoughts or regrets about my past choices in years. And now, all because of that jerk, the one-who-should-never-ever-be-named, I was thinking about that horrible time again. Eeeks. I needed to find new focus in life. For once I was grateful to EOFA for sending me to Shillong – hopefully, the clear blue skies, the verdant green, the pretty scenery of that beautiful place would clear my head of such unwarranted, unwelcome thoughts over the next two months. Thank you, EOFA.

7

Friday evening turned out to be a total anti-climax. Firstly, as I waited for Ankita to come back from work, my phone buzzed:

Hawkeye: Oindrilla, Sorry to disturb you. Have sent you a ppt. Take a look and make the changes I have outlined in the mail before Monday morning. Thx.

The phone beeped again!

Ankita: Hey, sorry, Tinku. I am going to be late. Some major gondogol on at work. Park Street plan kal subah subah. Promise. XXX

I had been composing a polite refusal to Hawkeye's message in my mind, when I read Ankita's. But if she was not coming back on time, why shouldn't I get done with this? (*Truth be told, I am a workaholic. A part of my fairly obsessive personality also doesn't let me relax if I know that work had to be done.*)

That was that then – I holed up in Ankita's room, pulled out my laptop and got done with the PPT and then fell fast asleep watching K-drama on Netflix. *I was glad that my Korean language skills were being put to use somewhere – even if it was to follow time-pass dramas.*

Sometime past 10:30 p.m., I woke up with a start. Ankita had tiptoed into the room and was taking out her nightclothes from the cupboard.

O: Hey you are back!

A: Oops, sorry, I tried not to make any noise. Sorry, di, I woke you up.

O: *Na, na, kichu* problem *noi*. Work issue resolved?

I sat up rubbing my eyes, and put aside the laptop. That was when I took a hard look at Ankita's face. No, no, not because I wanted to stare at her – but because I saw something that was strange. I squinted again, looked closer, simultaneously hunting for my specs which were somewhere on the bed (next to me / under me / wherever), with my hands.

"Tinku, what are you doing? You look strange! What a weird expression you have on your face." I must have looked weird, as I rummaged the bed with my hands looking for the pair of specs, while squinting at her.

Found it. The specs. Now I could see clearly again. Oh wait, what was wrong with Ankita's face? It looked puffed; her eyes were red.

"Hey, what happened? You have a fever? Your face looks puffed – as if you have been crying. Fuck! Have you been crying?"

Ankita glared at me. One solid, straight, stern glare. *Keep off. None of your business to meddle in* – the glare seemed to tell me. However, I was not the one to back down by these empty glares and threats. I persisted.

O: What happened?

A: Well, when you howled in the car, did I pester you? Leave me alone. I am fine.

O: Fine as fuck indeed. *Chhup kar*. Spill. When I howled in the car, please do note, the whole world – Ma, Mamu, driver, coolie, knew the reason. I demand that you tell me the reason why you are howling.

Since I was fairly persistent and stubborn when it came to getting to the source of the matter, I continued in this annoying vein in the hope that Ankita would spill. (Now, in most cases, I was an unobtrusive, grumpy person who prefers to let people be – annoying as they were – in their own stew. This was different. This was Ankita. Of all people why was SHE crying?)

Ankita, now clad in comfy pajamas, plonked herself on the bed, and coming close, jabbed me in the chest.

"Shhh! Will tell you tomorrow. The walls here have ears and I don't want the whole world to know. Have seen how mortified you were when the Vivek matter came out! *Owwwww...*"

It was my turn to jab her for triggering painful memories! Now, since curiosity (as to why Ankita was howling) was greater than mortification (when the whole world and their sisters found out about the V-matter), I let this pass with just a jab and decided to wait until the next day.

The night was long – longer than expected. For all her troubled, I-am-in-distress condition, Ankita fell asleep in flat two minutes and started snoring. On the other hand, the power nap earlier had refreshed me and I was unable to sleep. I therefore resumed my binge-watching. At some unearthly hour of the night, when the male protagonist finished killing everyone, I called it a day and my Friday came to a close.

***

"Tinku, Tinku!" I heard someone calling me from far, far away. Must be from somewhere in India, I was after all in a more interesting place. I was flying and I saw the tall skyscrapers of Gangnam beneath me. I was on my way to find Lee Min Ho

– ooh there he was – that was him. Looking so cool and swanky and cute as ever, he was atop a tall building, about to vanquish the evil hooded man in front of him. He turned just then, and saw me flying to his rescue, and smiled that cutie-pie grin … before turning into a fox! Fuck. Black Magic! That evil, hooded creep turned my (and several million others') LMH into a fox. I quickened my pace, and positioned myself to swoop down on that creep and vanquished him. He looked up, and revealed his sinister face and smiled. It was Vivek.

"TINKUUUUU GET UP!"

Ma was yelling in my ear, loudly! It was a mere dream, nay a nightmare. Back to reality – where I squinted and got showered with a seemingly never-ending volley of admonition.

It was 9:15 a.m. – I had overslept – and as per the rules at my *grandmother's* place, if one was not bathed and clean by 8:00 a.m., no breakfast was given. Why hadn't Ankita woken me up?

"Look at you, irresponsible girl. Look at Onkita; what a good girl. She helped Dida and Mami with the breakfast and other chores. Why do I even compare? All my fault – for pampering you silly."

Hein, when? I did more than my share of housework back home in Delhi. Who made breakfast/lunch/dinner when the maid was not there – which was perpetually the case? I was too sleepy (and dazed) to protest and argue; so, I tucked in my tail (*even though Vivek had turned LMH into a fox; not me*) and scurried into the bathroom!

8

"Ma, Ankita and I are going out."

"No, Dida, we won't be back for lunch."

"No, we aren't meeting anyone. Just the two of us. No, Mami, not shopping."

"And no, we are not going to Flury's."

Good heavens. The flurry of questions would just not stop. It felt like school days again – when Dida and Mami had to know about our plans and whereabouts. Ma never had much time – so while she would not interrogate like the other two ladies, she would sneakily get the details out.

By the time the cab got to Mamu's place, the three women had charted our itinerary for the day. Why, Ankita and I stood like dumb ducks and listened to that was another matter altogether. Despite my grumpy exterior which makes people think that I was a rebel, the truth was that I could never say no to parents/grandparents/bosses/authority figures. And despite Ankita's goody-goody exterior, she could be decisive and assertive and could say no. However, she was surprisingly quiet and lost. Something was definitely bothering her. Work shouldn't and hadn't distracted my efficient cousin ever before.

"Anku, *ki holo? Kicchu* problem?"

Ankita was staring at her phone as she directed the *Bihari* cab *wala* where to go.

"*Na*, nothing."

Very strange. Curt replies weren't her thing either. I didn't bother probing further in most cases, simply because I didn't want people butting in on my affairs. But this was my cousin – my baby sister. A sudden swell of mushy, maternal feelings (hitherto unknown to me) surfaced and I hugged Ankita.

"Don't worry, baby, your work will get better," I patted Ankita's back.

"*Hein*, Tinku Di! Get off me! Get off me!" She pushed back – almost as if I were molesting her.

"*Sab theek hai,* madam? Is this lady troubling you? Should I call the police?" The annoying Bihari cab driver stopped the cab to check.

WTF! I cannot even explain what I went through at that moment. My sisterly concern had been misinterpreted for an assault by the cabbie. A moustached, tough-looking bugger, was glaring at me, and was ready to get me arrested.

"*Arre*, no, no, I am her cousin. *Aap chalaiye.*" Fuck, why did I have to explain? What was my stupid cousin up to? Why was she not coming to my defence? *Uff*! She was again staring at her phone.

"Ankuuuuuuuuu!"

She stirred from her reverie – high time at that – and looked up rather dazed. "*Haan haan, bhaiyya, chaliye.*"

Once the Bihari cabbie with the big *moochh* was kind of convinced that I wasn't molesting Ankita, he started the cab again and we were finally on our way to Park Street. I was now completely in a bad mood – what with the cabbie shooting me regular glares through the rear-view mirror and my cousin looking at her phone with glazed eyes.

I did what I did best in such situations – dozed off.

"Tinku Di, get up. We are here."

***

"*Ahhhhhh*. Tinku, what are you doing?"

The first thing I did on getting out of the cab was to whack her!

How dare she let me be so bloody humiliated? Here I was, concerned and worried about her glazed eyes and overall trauma and there she let me be mistaken for a molester!

"What is wrong with you? That fucking cabbie thought I was molesting you. Yikes! And you? You just kept quiet! WHAAT IS WRONG?"

My mini outburst on a crowded Park Street had some effect. Other than passers-by staring at me, that is. The prim-n-propah Ankita was back! Grabbing me by the shoulder, she dragged me into the nearest café she could spot.

I kept quiet till we were seated and our orders had been placed. That girl had started staring at the fucking phone again with glazed eyes. Seriously, man, even I was not married to my phone that much. The phone needed to go and I snatched it from her.

"What are you doing, Tinku Di?"

"You tell me, young lady. You have been behaving strangely since yesterday. You also have gotten married to this phone – and are staring at it with gooey-gooey eyes. Pathetic. Spill! Now!"

Thankfully, Ankita looked a bit shame-faced. "Tinku Di, I am in trouble. I am in love."

"What the fuck!"

"Mind your language. There is nothing to be shocked about."

"Why would I be shocked about your falling in love? Every other year, since the time you turned 13, you have been in love with one or the other. Wasn't there that Mukherjee boy that you were dating?

"Then what?"

"You have had that glazed, harassed-dying-duck-look the past two days. You want me to bash up someone for you?"

Make no mistake, people. Despite my size – pint sized, I admit, I have awesome kick-ass Taekwondo skills, which I would proudly show off any day, provided I got the chance. This sounded way too tempting an opportunity.

"Are you mad, Tinku Di? Did you not hear me? I am in love."

"I heard. You are in love. Ok, Great! But why this dying-duck expression then? I don't get it. Explain."

Ankita looked at me, with that expression back in her eyes, and sighed.

Why did I land up in cafes these days to listen to other people's love confessions? First it was Sweety and now it was Ankita. Oh, I needed to check with Sweety – it had been three days and the gal hadn't even bothered to message/call me. Too much – the lovesick people and their idiosyncracies. Thank God, I was OK. In fact, it had been too long since I dated. I required a replacement boyfriend to dispel any unwelcome, unpleasant thoughts about the jerk-who-never-shall-be-named. Oh, Anku was asking me something and here I had completely zoned off.

"Yes, Anku. So, what's the problem?" I crooned, with a sweet smile trying to cover up the fact that I had heard fuck-all.

"Huh, what problem? I just told you – I am in love. Prabhas and I are mad about each other. *Bas*."

"Then why have you been sulking the past two days? Who is Prabhas? Details please!"

"Where have I been sulking? It's called being preoccupied. Prabhas and I were having a minor argument about a small matter. Well, Prabhas is my boyfriend – the love of my life," saying so the gal went back to mooning over her phone.

"Where did you meet this guy, Prabhas? North Indian? Doesn't sound Bangla to me. What does the name mean? What happened to Indrajit? The Mukherjee man, the one you were snogging when Mamu caught you? Why did you break up with Indrajit? Does Prabhas know about Indrajit?"

It was a one-sided conversation. I volleyed all the above questions, dug into my plate, and waited for answers – which never came. No response.

"Is he a *ch***iya*? This Prabhas?"

"Tinku Di, stop it! *Chup koro tumi*."

Finally at last. Yay. She heard me. She had not gone deaf. With that the conversation was over. Now, I know this girl. Something was wrong – no matter what she said.

I went back to polishing my plate and Anku to her phone.

Her only contribution to this so-called conversation was – "What else?"

Then when I would ask a question, there was absolute, radio pin-drop silence!

"Anku, did I tell you? Sweety came out last week!"

No response.

"*Arre*, you aren't even reacting to this. Stop looking at your phone and talk to me."

"What is there to react? You and Sweety Di meet every week; so you went out and got wasted in another pub / bar, big deal! I know, I am a bit pre-occupied. Give me a few minutes, please, please." She smiled that sweet pleading smile of hers, the one I could never resist, and I left it at that.

I continued fiddling with my spoon as I waited for her to get done. We might as well as have gone home and I could get back to my K-drama world. Since patience was not one of my strongest virtues and instant self-gratification was what I actively pursued, I pulled out my phone, plugged in my earphones and logged on to Netflix.

Just when I was about to lose myself in Lee Min Ho's cute charms, I heard a deep, low, attractive and very familiar voice behind me.

"Why, isn't that Oindrilla? Again? My luck must be shining. I get to meet you twice in three days."

Holy fuck. Vivek.

I looked up in absolute horror, torn between the drama on screen and the drama about to unfurl in my real life.

***

Ankita, that bitch, now put her phone down and cooed.

"Hello, Vivek Da. Not sure if you remember me. I am Ankita, her cousin."

"I do, Ankita. You are all grown-up now. So good to meet you," replied Vivek, warmly hugging her and proceeding to seat himself at our table.

I was not at my finest best of course. For a few minutes, I don't think I did anything other than gawp at him like a dying duck. Then I regained my senses.

"Hello Vivek. Who asked you to sit down? Don't you have anything better to do? Just go away."

He smiled. Oh shit, the smile had gotten more lethal than what I remembered. He got up and walked away. Phew.

"Anku, now we must leave," I hissed.

"*Arre*, I am yet to get done with this."

"Shove your fucking phone in your bag and gulp it down. We have to leave."

"Leave? Not so soon, Oindrilla. Do have a cup of tea with me also," Vivek had come back.

Noooooo. Why on earth did he have to look, sound and smell so good? Why am I such a bloody idiot?

What the bloody hell. Anku suddenly was at her sweetest best, cooing to the jerk, and forgot all about lover boy Prabhas. I glared repeatedly, tried to catch her attention, but I was royally ignored.

"Why, Oindrilla? You don't look too happy to see me. Considering we were such good friends back in our school days, one would think you would be delighted to see me. I am. Totally thrilled to have met you again. Happy to see you also, Ankita."

Vivek. The smart ass! To think I fancied myself in *saccha pyaar* with him – for all these years. I wanted to throw something on his head right away.

"Vivek, why would you think I would be happy to see you? Especially after what happened?" I blurted out, recovering my tongue at last.

Ankita's phone rang. Phew, that was timely … for her. It probably was the lover boy Prabhas calling. Madam quickly excused herself, requested me to foot the bill and go home on my own. She then cooed a goodbye to Vivek and scooted.

All in less than two minutes, even before I could utter a word in protest.

There I was, staring at my phone. *Basically, to avoid looking at the bloody jerk, who was literally staring at me.*

"Vivek, surely you have a life and something better to do. Will you stop staring at me and just fuck off?"

"Oh, the motor mouth, everything intact, you still are the same."

The jerk drawled in such a deep sexy voice that it did all sorts of things to my bloody disloyal heart and turned my toes … Aargh. *Everything intact? What the fuck does he even mean?*

"I don't get what it is that you want from me, Vivek. Since you just refuse to take hints, here I say it again – Go away from here and leave me alone."

"Ah those fiery, flashing eyes. Always impulsive, now it seems you have become stupid as well. Well done. Kolkata is not what it used to be. Spending extended periods of time with you isn't my cup of tea either. I don't want to read a news item tomorrow that screams – 'CRAZY LADY FROM DELHI BEATS UP A POOR CAB DRIVER'!"

"What bullshit! I can get back on my own. Without beating up anyone or getting beaten up. Huh!"

So much for his fake concern. Exactly what degree of an idiot was I? Here I was, having butterflies in my heart because my disloyal ex-crush and could-have-been-boyfriend from the past, had offered to drop me home. Facepalm! No, no, face to the bloody wall.

"Look, let's get this over with. Your uncle's place? Same one?"

I nodded curtly and we got moving. As we came out on to the crowded street, the evening sky was lit in a pink hue and dark clouds bunching together had made an appearance.

"You stay put here. I will be back with my car," saying this the man walked away in a hurry. I was left with a strange sense of déjà vu, or whatever you called this fucked-up feeling.

I, Oindrilla Roy, all of 26-years-old, was standing at exactly the same spot (ok ok, not exactly the same spot but the same street), where I had been unceremoniously dumped (ok, ok, not dumped as such – I mean, he didn't say that or anything but I got my heart broken into a million places, hence) by the very same guy (who had just left to get his car from the parking).

What am I doing? Ankita, you have a lot to pay for this. Just so that you could run to your lover boy Prabhas, you left me with the devil. Fuck. My. Life.

Now, instead of doing something heroic (read foolhardy) and leaving on my own, I stood there, waiting for the jerk, with a large scowl on my face. I didn't know whom I wanted to whack more – Ankita, Vivek or myself!

"Good, I didn't let you go alone in a cab," Vivek remarked, as I seated myself in the car and pulled on the seat belt.

I looked up, scowling a bit more. It had started pouring now.

Since I did not see any need to be even polite or considerate, I continued scowling. Misinterpreting my disdainful, pissed-off look to be a questioning one, he continued with the same old poor joke, "Can't let you go alone and endanger a poor cab *wallah*, considering the mood you are in!"

"If you don't shut up, I will murder you, Vivek."

He chuckled. Idiot me. There was no reason for me to fall for the bait, but still I had. But better sense prevailed and I put on my headphones and started listening to music. I did not wish to converse or get provoked. I didn't even want to be dropped home. He had taken upon this driver duty himself.

Luckily, he took the hint as well and kept quiet. The rest of the journey was thus spent in cold, stony silence. I was relieved to get out of the car and bid him a curt goodbye. Thank God, I was off to Shillong the next day.

"Stay safe and be happy, Oindrilla."

"You too, Vivek."

I forced a smile as I wished him well and was relieved to get back home. For the past however many years, I had wondered (often, sadly) what I would do if I ever got to meet Vivek again. Now that I actually did, I was quite impressed with myself. For I didn't burst into tears, yell at him (oh I did that a bit, but come on, that was more being rude) and did not launch into a tirade about what had happened back then. *Oindrilla Roy, be proud of yourself ... and Ankita, you are dead!*

9

Ankita would be dead, if she were home.

"*Eta abar ki*? Where is *Onkita*?" Ma looked up from her laptop as I walked into the house!

Shoot! The girl had not yet gotten back from her tryst with lover boy Prabhas.

"Oh, I don't know. She got a phone call and then she left. She said she would get back on her own," I muttered, flummoxed. I was a terrible liar and especially in front of Ma. For all my belligerence and devil-may-care attitude (which was bloody put-on anyway), I was shit scared of Ma! One look from her and all the *sach* came out. Anyway, this wasn't a blatant lie. Ankita did leave me alone and said she would get back on her own.

Phew, Ma didn't pry, for at that very moment, both our phones pinged with the same message.

Urgent. Video call NOW. No excuses!

From Baba.

"Now what has that man done? One day alone, and he can't stay without getting into trouble."

Ma grumbled as she tore herself from her laptop. She was being rather reluctant to leave the laptop in the first place. Was she working as she proclaimed to be or watching something on Netflix as I had been doing? Moving closer to her laptop, I sneaked a peek at the screen to see what Ma was upto. Damn, no Netflix. Momentarily, I felt the joy at possibly catching Ma doing something naughty, which then could have been leveraged at *sudhaaroing* my own *jeevan*!

She seemed to be struggling with some power point presentation – making it, that is.

***

My parents, as adorable that they are, are also senior bureaucrats – which meant that they had *hazaar* people in their office and homes to do their bidding. One person to make PPTs, one person to hold the mouse, one person to answer emails, one person to make *chai*. So on and so forth.

"We have to call Baba," I reminded her.

"Oh yes, I forgot."

Hein, how was that even possible? She had typed one word in the past five minutes. Well, whatever. As I picked up my phone to call, it rang. Baba was video calling! This must be bad, given that he had called instead of waiting for us.

"Babaaaaaa..."

"TINKU, stop squealing. It has only been two days since you last saw him." *Ma, always the spoilsport, was still glaring at her laptop, perhaps trying to type word no. 2*!

"Baba, *ki holo*?"

"*Arre, betu*, we are in BIG trouble."

"Did you burn the house, Ranjan?" *Ma in her sternest voice, still typing word no. 2.*

Baba shook his head, as if on cue. He was one trained husband, being so used to responding to Ma's orders. Even though he couldn't see her, he was answering listening to her voice!

"Tinku, where is Ma?"

"Right here, behind me, Baba. I think she is trying to get her laptop to do something. But her special glares, which work on us, aren't working on the laptop!"

"Ok, Tinku, Meeta (if you are listening, which you definitely will be), we have a crisis at home."

"Now, Ranjan, will you stop repeating the same thing in different sentences? Get to the matter."

"Ok, something terrible happened this morning. I could not even go to the office."

"WHAT?" Ma and I both screamed in unison. This suspense was now killing us.

"I had taken Choco and Chipki for a walk. Those stupid dogs."

"RANJAN," Ma stood up. The ppt was forgotten promptly.

"Stupid, only, Meeta. Listen to what happened. That Makkhan Singh came in their view, and both got excited. They barked and barked. Usually, Tinku helps in controlling one dog; today she was not there. Choco ran away. Chipki fought with Makkhan and they mauled each other. Both are with the animal authorities now."

"What? One day I am not there and this happens?" Ma wailed in a most dramatic fashion.

"Baba, what did you do then? Did you try looking for Choco?"

"Oh I did. Thankfully, she found her way back to the house. Meeta, I have spoken to the Director there. We should be able to bring Chipki back but those buggers are suing us."

"WHAT? WHO?" – yelled Ma and I, again in unison.

"The people to whom Makkhan Singh belongs."

"Why?"

"They said that our Chipki attacked and injured Makkhan Singh first." "Makkhan Singh died?" I asked, suddenly sorry for that ferocious beast!

Baba glared at me. "Had he died, those uncouth people would have gotten me arrested."

"Arrested? Are you calling from jail then, Ranjan?"

"Meeta, are you now hard of hearing as well? Comprehension was always a bit of an issue," muttered Baba under his breath.

The lioness in Ma had awakened; her Choco, Chipki and her beloved husband (in that order) were in danger in her absence.

"I leave you for one day and you make such a mess of things. Tinku, reschedule my tickets for tomorrow morning. I will leave at 10 a.m. tomorrow," Ma proclaimed, causing everyone to gasp.

You see, we had yelled so much that by now Dida, Mamu and Mami had all gathered to watch the Roy family comedy show. And now the collective gasp was asking just one question.

Was Meeta Roy, also known as Ma to me, mad? She was booked on a late afternoon flight the next day any which way.

"But Ma, you are taking the 4 p.m. flight back," I added, in a low tone, not wanting to get my head bitten off.

"Meeta, you are coming back tomorrow evening!" Baba, a daring man, said at the same time.

"So? I do not wish to come back in the evening to be told that the obnoxious Singhs have fed my Choco to Makkhan Singh!"

"Is that Makkhan Singh a dog or a lion, Di?" Mamu decided to butt in. Seriously the level of conversation in my household didn't surprise me anymore. It was exactly as weird as we were.

It was at this moment, thankfully, that the Roy family's conversation came to an end. For Ankita entered, eliciting such sharp reactions that Ma's attention was diverted. Only attention mind you. No mere mortal could distract her from her intention. Ma's unilateral decision to go by the 10 a.m. flight instead of the 4 p.m. flight was upheld ... later.

"Ankuuuuu, where were you?" I squealed like a fool, when I spotted her at the front door. Quite an idiot – that was me for the time being. I had no clue that the entire family would *barso* on her.

"Tinku, wasn't Anku with you? I had seen you both leave together." That was Mamu.

"Anku, you left Tinku all alone and went off somewhere else? Tinku, how did you get back home? And where were you?" Dida at her loudest.

Mami, by now used to the loud Mukherjee-Roy family, was the only quiet one other than Baba (still on video, with a rather disinterested look). Poor Baba, on one side the loud Sikhs and on the other, the loud Mukherjees – some choice that! He had tried to get Ma to cut the call but Anku's entry and the noise that followed blocked his fervent pleas.

"*Arre*, I am home, well within the curfew time. Tinku is older than me; she knows the city and she is back home safe and sound. Don't know what the issue is." *My family had a curfew time. And we followed it. Such was life.*

10

The Mukherjee household was in a state of utter chaos the next morning, which was Sunday. Please note – most of the noise was being made by Ma and me, with some help from Dida. Dida, the darling she is, was fussing over *me* – keep this, keep that. It felt good to be fussed over for a change.

Since the previous night, Ma had called Baba some 15 times – checking on Choco and Chipki and inquiring whether the obnoxious Singhs had landed at her doorstep to torture her family again!

"Meeta, its past midnight. No, the Singhs haven't and will not come. You meet them tomorrow when you get here. Now let me sleep."

"Sleep? This is a crisis. My Chipki is still not home and those Singhs are still at large. Ranjan, how come you are sleeping?"

"What can the Singhs do now? Chipki is safe, and fine. She will be home tomorrow."

"What can the Singhs do? Ranjan, they are Punjabis! I tell you; they are not at all to be trusted. They can do anything! How can you sleep?"

"Ma, I want to sleep. Speak softly," I butted in. This was disturbing.

"*Uff*, Tinku, always bothered about yourself. Selfish. Extremely abominable! Well, I have brought you up – you are our only child. Hence my fault!"

"Ma."

"Meeta."

"MEETA, STOP SPEAKING SO LOUDLY. THERE ARE OTHER PEOPLE IN THE HOUSE WHO ARE TRYING TO SLEEP." (Dida finally came to the rescue!)

Thank God for Dida. Ma stopped her tirade and cut the call and tried to sleep – for some time. She perhaps called again – but by then I was in la la land, visiting Seoul for my next instalment of Lee Min Ho.

***

The car ride to the airport in the morning was rather interesting. Ma was in the front seat, latching on to her phone, and checking on Chipki and the Singhs every ten minutes! *God, Ma has an obsessive streak in her ... Maybe I have it too. We are a nutty family!*

Ankita sat glued to her phone. Poor Mamu, silent and stoic as ever, was focussed on the road ahead. As I restlessly looked here and there, my phone beeped.

Sorry, Tinku, I have been distracted. Planning to come to Shillong to meet you one of these days. Will explain. Don't squeal. Reply by message only!

Huh?? Why was Ankita messaging me? She was sitting right next to me.

Don't squeal or react. REPLY BY MESSAGE. CONTROL.

That was Ankita again. On WA. She figured I was about to excitedly ask her why. I controlled myself successfully and did not squeal.

Ankita, what is going on? All this is making me extremely curious.

Bad times in relationship, Tinku Di.

What relationship? The only relationship you have is with your phone!

I told you about Prabhas, no?

Oh, yes. Lover boy Prabhas. What happened yesterday?

Later, later, Tinku Di. Next weekend, perhaps.

Next weekend? You plan to come to Shillong? Yay.

Maybe. Ok, bye. The folks in the front seat will notice that something's up. Talk later.

So, this is how my Kolkata stopover ended once Ma and I were deposited at the airport – by a silent Mamu and a preoccupied Ankita.

***

By the time, Ma and I completed the security check at the airport for our respective flights, I was at my wit's end. Ma, I did love her; but she was also extremely annoying. Barely had I bid goodbye to her (we were in different gates and boarding was to commence shortly), and reached the gate, I got a frantic call from her.

"Tinkuuuuu, *amaar* iPad *kothai*?"

"*Kothai maane*? You had it with you. You were looking moonfully at Choco and Chipki's pics, remember?"

"Come and find it now!" She ordered.

Shit. I had no choice but to head back towards Ma's gate to figure out where she had put the iPad. So, the hunt began

– I looked in her bags, the loo, the nearby table, and almost everywhere else. The iPad was nowhere to be found.

"Tinku … security check. I left it there!" Ma remembered.

I found myself soon in the security check area, trying to get someone's attention so that the iPad could be retrieved.

"Excuse me, Sir. My mother had probably left her iPad on this baggage belt some time back. *Aapko mila kya*?" (Me at my politest best…)

"No madam, I don't remember."

"Oh, could you please look," I requested again politely. How I wished I could flutter my eyelashes and turn on some charm.

Fortunately for me, the other CISF officer on duty remembered an abandoned iPad.

"Oho, it must have been that one which the bomb squad examined."

"*Arre, haan*, Madam, your iPad is with the bomb squad!"

FUCK! Now I had to locate the bomb squad guys. The kind CISF officers pointed me to a shady-looking office somewhere near the baggage belt. As I hurried towards the office, worried that I would miss my flight, I bumped straight into a tallish gentleman and found myself and my handbag being hurled to the ground.

"I am sorry. I was in a hurry, ma'am. May I please help you?" crooned the deep, helpful and very familiar voice. Mollified, I looked up, all set to bestow a grateful smile at the owner of the voice…

"Not a problem … it is … YOU? AGAIN? Are you following me, Vivek Rao?"

"Oindrilla, I should have known. No other civilized woman would have flung herself at me." Vivek was also not too happy to see me. He was frowning.

"Get off me. I am in a hurry," I squealed.

"I am not on top of you. You are sprawled on the floor and need to pick yourself up. Kindly get up and go your own way."

Saying this, the bloody jerk just walked away. Why on earth did I have to meet Vivek Rao each time when I was so not prepared? Since I did not have much time, I did not obsess on this topic (anyway, I had the whole flight to do so) and wisely ran to the bomb squad people to locate the iPad.

"iPad, you said, ma'am?"

"Yes, Sir. My mother left her iPad on the baggage belt at the security check point. I am trying to locate it. I was informed that it was with you."

"Hmm, your name and boarding card, please. And your mother's also. You are saying that the iPad is hers. Where is she?"

"Huh, oh Ma is at the gate. You need her boarding card as well?"

In short, I found myself caught up in a massively frustrating bureaucratic rigmarole. They started asking me to fill forms in triplicate; furnish identity proofs (both mine and my mother's) and that they would like to see her in person! *Why were they looking at me so strangely? As though I had some criminal record! Buck up, Oinks.*

"Madam, your name please."

"Again, this is the third time I am telling you my name, address, etc., etc. What more details do you need? That is my iPad and I WANT IT BACK."

I had also had enough – of being stared at with such suspicion. But my loud outburst got me surrounded by three security personnel. Fuck. Had I become a security threat? They were looking at me as if I were some suicide bomber about to set off bombs on my mission. Smartly, I adopted a placatory tone and pleaded with them to get my iPad back.

A senior officer entered the room and asked me the same bloody questions. *Don't these people exchange notes*?

"Look, Sir, sorry, but my Ma left her iPad by mistake and I am here to collect it."

"How do we know it's yours? How do we know you have a Ma? Please produce her!"

I called Ma.

"Ma, you are needed here. NOW."

"For what? You can't fetch a simple iPad?"

"I am at the bomb squad office. They want you to come here and testify that it's your iPad. Also, they don't seem to believe me at all."

"Who is the officer-in-charge?" The bureaucrat in Ma had woken up. She was pulling out her secret weapon.

I read out the name of the person asking me those *hazaar* questions. She asked me to pass on the phone to him, which I duly did.

"Yes, ma'am... So...rry, ma'am. No no, please don't worry. Yes, ma'am."

Ma had pulled rank on him. Yay, for that. I got the iPad back.

Thankfully – in one shape and piece. It even switched on. Thank the one above! Else Ma would have made me purchase an iPad right then and there at the airport – and pay for it.

Handing over the iPad to her, I rushed to my gate – barely making it in time for the boarding announcement.

I joined the snaky, long queue, wondering rather seriously about the number of people who were travelling to Shillong. Wasn't it a sleepy small town? Why was the whole world going there anyway? Such serious thoughts, definitely an improvement over what usually passes through my mind, were interrupted.

"Oindrilla, again! One would think you are following me, my dear."

Oh God. Vivek again. He was right behind me. Now why was this bloody jerk going to Shillong?

"Do you have nowhere else to go? Why Shillong?"

"Now that's my girl. Blunt and rude as ever."

I ignored his taunt and started focussing on the long, curvy line ahead. Now why was this line not moving? The longer we stood still, the more Vivek would try conversing, the more there was a risk that I would hit him on the head and get arrested for assault.

Patience, Oinks, Patience.

"Why, Oindrilla, is it written somewhere that I should not travel to Shillong?"

There. Vivek was trying to provoke me again. Damn, the bloody jerk knew exactly what buttons to press. I was too pissed to even fall for it though.

"Will you stop staring at me?"

"You look so hassled. What happened, Oindrilla? Did you go on a tumbling spree again?" The jerk chuckled, at his very own poor joke.

"None of your bloody business. Stop staring at me and mind your business."

"Aha a bad, bad mood. Not that I wish to get involved in your business, Ciao."

"Aww that hurt." Shit. How did that come out of my mouth?

"Come again. Did I hear you right?" *Of course, Vivek the fucking Rao would latch onto this and torment me for as long as he could!*

"Yes, I am upset and bloody pissed. You aren't making my life any less easy," *Woah. I didn't know who was more surprised at my frank admission. Before I could react and put the other foot in my mouth, thankfully the line started moving. Shit. Making an ass, a complete ass of myself, was a skill I was a pro at.*

The phone rang. Not mine, Vivek's. Despite the pissed-off state of mind I found myself in – thanks to Ma's iPad and stupid CISF officer, my *bacha-kucha* brain functioned and I used this as an excuse to hurriedly try and get away. Not giving that man any chance to probe any further. *Shut up, Oinks. Don't go pouring out your heart to a jerk who broke it eons ago. He is not a friend. (But he was – my best friend.) THAT SHIP SAILED A LONG TIME AGO.*

"Hey Oindrilla, it is you. Didn't realise that Zarine had booked us on the same flight from Kolkata," The lady I was trying to get past, as I escaped from Vivek, happened to be none than NBA. *Oh god, no, no, no, what rotten luck.*

"Oh hi, Aparna, sorry, didn't see you. Was in a bit of a hurry."

"Not at all an issue. Which seat are you in? I am in 5 E."

"5 D" *Oh brilliant, I have to sit next to NBA through the flight. Bas Hawkeye is missing...*

My phone beeped just then. *Yay, I have an excuse to not to speak to NBA.*

Sweety: Hey, Oinks, where you? No call-shall, no messages, nothing. Where?

Now, ever since Sweety told me about the bitch Divya, I hadn't even texted her. It was definitely not intentional. Oh God, what must she think of me? A closet homophobe? How could I forget to message Sweety? She was my dear, dearer, dearest friend. It was all that bloody Vivek's fault and Ankita's confused love story.

Feeling rather remorseful at my own thoughtless behaviour (and bugged some more at Vivek), I decided I would call her once I reach Shillong. Now a more urgent matter needed my focus and attention. How was I to *jhelo* this strange NBA – who was neither making an attempt to be overly bitchy nor overly friendly – as we stood in the boarding queue.

From the corner of my eye, I peeked at her. She was on her phone, typing some messages rather brutally. Boy, one of her moods perhaps – bitching about someone. Perhaps me? *Bah, Oinks, you are not that important. Shut it.*

I looked behind to see how long the queue was. Ok, that was a lie. I wanted to check whether Vivek was really on this flight or had he given me that bit of info to vex me. Damn! Vivek was very much there. Laughing ever so charmingly. He was speaking to a tall, gangly, model-type lady next to him. All that charm was turned on for impressing her? Hmm.

Was she his girlfriend? Then what happened to Shreya? My curiosity started to get the better of me. I started thinking of ways, not so obvious, of course, to verify that fact. Since that certainly was not possible, I decided to look in front. Idiot me. Not Vivek. How stupid could I be? He broke my heart into hundred-thousand-gazillion pieces and walked away (*Ok I walked away! Without letting him explain or speaking to him*) and here I was still sneaking looks at the same guy after so many years. Pathetic. Where were Sweety or Ankita when I needed them? Bah, one was with Divya and the other with lover boy Prabhas.

Focus, Oinks, Focus! Phew. The line started moving and finally we got on the flight.

11

It turned out that not only had Zarine booked NBA and me on the same flight, she had even checked us in together – in adjacent seats! As I sat down and placed my laptop bag in the overhead bin, my phone beeped. It was Zarine.

Z: *Heylo heylo. On the flight? Met Aparna and Rahul? Have a safe flight.* ☻

Fuck. Hawkeye also on the same flight? Nightmare only. I noted with alarm that the aisle seat in our row was empty. NBA had already made herself comfortable. She was still typing furiously on her phone. Boy! She was either angry or that was the way she typed. Fast and furious … I was staring at her and got caught! Wonder of wonders! She smiled at me. Holy shit.

"Do you always type so fast, Aparna?" I blurted out thoughtlessly. *Why on earth do I never ever think*?

She laughed. "Yes, I do. Quite brutal, no? That's what Vipin says."

"Vipin?"

"My husband."

I smiled, sat down and took out my phone to put it on flight mode. I did not fancy cooing to NBA and perhaps even

Hawkeye (when and if he showed up) and wondered what to do. Oh yes, Netflix to the rescue. I shouldn't have bothered. NBA was also not too keen to chat with me. She pulled out her Kindle (Oh she reads. That's interesting info) and was into it. There was no sign of Hawkeye when we took off (NBA did not mention anything to me about him). Vivek the jerk, along with that tall, gangly, fucking-Miss was also not in my vicinity, so I got lost in the fantasy world of Lee Min Ho – my King!

By the time we landed at the Umroi Airport, I had plodded through two rather painful and slow episodes of the show. Painful only because of my own fucking mind. I was too distracted. It was Vivek the jerk who was getting under my skin. The thought that Hawkeye and NBA could be present at what might be my weakest moment was not encouraging either. Hence, at several points in time during the flight, Lee Min Ho was conveniently forgotten as I looked out of the window and wool-gathered!

***

The view outside was breathtaking, Shillong was an absolute delight to the senses. I forgot both Vivek the jerk and his gangly miss. For a while. Why, I was even kindly disposed to Hawkeye and NBA.

"Wow, this is lovely," NBA intruded into my reverie. What reverie. My mind was blank – as was the case most of the fricking time.

"Yes, it is," I replied. I was feeling happy and strangely peaceful to wish to appear rude.

"Rahul was on this flight too. Guess we will meet him at the baggage belt. We can then take a cab to our hotel."

"Oh, is that so? Cool."

"This does look like it will be a good trip, Oindrilla. Is this your first time to Shillong?" Aparna said, smiling very kindly.

She is being nice to me. Or is she taking a dig? I nodded wordlessly, almost embarrassed.

"My first time too. I do want to look around. Hmm... You know what? Let's take a day off post that meeting with the clients. Maybe on Wednesday. I have made a list of all the tourist spots to visit. Why don't you come with me?" Aparna pitched in enthusiastically.

Uh, what was going on? She was being nice to me. As I continued to stare at her, with an absolutely zapped expression on my idiotic face – probably part constipated, part-agonized, she patted me gently on my shoulder.

"Oindrilla, if you are worried about Rahul agreeing to a day off especially since you had taken a few days off recently, don't be. I will speak to him."

Finally, I remembered that I could speak and muttered a hurried, "Thank you. OK. OK, please." I wasn't agonized because NBA was nice to me or that I had to ask Hawkeye for yet another leave. I could already visualise him, saying in his uniquely, irritating nasal high-pitched voice, "*Oiiindrillla, chhutti? Phir se? he he he.*" NBA could and would get me the required permissions. That I was not the least bit bothered about.

I was agonized because this conversation took place when we were getting our luggage from the overhead cabin. As I was in the process of doing so, I spotted the-jerk-who-should-never-be-named looking charming, and listening (intently at that) to that tall, svelte companion of his; his sunshine crinkly smile had lit up his face as that dame cosied up to him. Fuck. He was charming. Even more so now. And

I was pathetic. *Oindrilla Roy – get a bloody life. Go sightseeing with NBA and feel better.*

Regaining my composure at last, I chimed in, "Thanks, Aparna. If you can convince Hawk … oops Rahul, I am in." *Shit. I almost called him Hawkeye*! That too in front of NBA. I tried looking rather nonchalant and walked straight ahead and fell in with the moving file. Lucky escape! Phew! Or so I thought.

"By the way, Oindrilla, what did you refer to Rahul as?" Aparna asked, curiously 10 minutes later. *Shit.* She had not forgotten. Aparna and I were standing at the baggage belt, waiting for our luggage to show up. I was focussed on glaring and shooting mental daggers aimed at the back of you-know-who. He was standing a few feet away, still engrossed in that tall dame's endless conversation, and was blocking my view. I couldn't see my luggage, thanks to their annoying selves clouding my vision and their unnecessary loud laughter blocking my ears! *Oinks, idiot, you don't have a singing suitcase. Get a grip and handle the earlier goof-up first!*

"Ha ha (embarrassed laughter) Tejas and I have a nickname for him." *Handling a goof-up doesn't mean that you confess the bloody truth. Now what if she goes and tells him?* It was in times like these, that I missed having Sweety or Tejas near me. Sweety – everywhere and Tejas – at office. They would have glibly covered their faux pas up. Not gawk like me.

Aparna smiled. "Hawk, is it? That's what you kids call him? Suits him. He does swoop down upon you all like a hawk." *Huh Huh. WHAT IS GOING ON?* "It's ok. I won't tell him. Isn't that one yours?" She continued, pointing towards the baggage carousel, where a bright orange suitcase (yes, mine), was making its way towards us. I picked it up and moved a bit behind, slightly away from the rest of the travellers. NBA was still waiting for hers. Since she had been nice so far, I couldn't just walk away. I stood at a distance and started scrolling through my unread Whatsapp messages, while waiting for her to show up.

"Oindrilllaaaa, *aa gayi tum*?" yelled Rahul aka Hawkeye my boss. Only he could say such an inane thing. We were both supposedly on the same flight! Still in this moment, it was better to be nice to him than stare at the bane of my life!

"*Haan*, how was your flight?" I beamed at him, "I did not see you." Hawkeye smiled and was about to say something when his phone blared, its sharp ring tone loud and clear. "Sorry, Boss *ka hai*." As he stepped aside to suck up to Boss, I looked back at the belt to see where NBA was. What was taking her so long? Oh shit! Aparna was speaking to Vivek and that tall, gangly girl he was stuck to! They were all coming this side. To where I was standing. I quickly went back to scrolling through my messages, which were now all read! *Why oh why does this happen to me? Calm down, Oinks. Grow up. You are NOT a pathetic 17-year-old. Behave your age. Besides, the honeymooning couple will soon be off on their own way and then you can deal with NBA.*

I was ready to face the world and the blasted Vivek again.

"There you are. Oindrilla, meet Vivek and Ishita. They are from Price Waterhouse Coopers. Will be working on the same implementation as us. Oh yes, they are putting up at Hotel Rosewood as well."

"Hi, most pleased to meet you, Oin … Oindrilla, is it? Nice name! I am Vivek Rao," Vivek smiled, turning all the charm on. That was a first!

Slimeball. As if he didn't know my name. Jerk!

"Nice meeting you. Vivek. Hello, Ishita. Look forward to working with you both."

Behaving like a complete grown-up, I did not roll my eyes, or stick out my tongue or punch him. Instead, I smiled sweetly at both of them.

I was spared any further conversation post this. What with Hawkeye jumping in and taking charge of the entire conversation and situation. Before he launched off into a high-pitched nasal monologue about the said implementation that we were all assembled in Shillong for, Aparna smartly intervened and suggested we go to the hotel and check in. Work talk could be conducted over breakfast the next day. Tejas was right. Aparna was not all that bad!

***

As we parted ways at the airport to head to the same bloody hotel, and made our way to the taxi stand, I realised I had dropped my ear phones somewhere – probably near the baggage belt where we were standing and cooing! I told NBA and Hawkeye about the matter and decided to go look for them. This would have been possible if only they would let me back into the airport. The security guard at the gate stared at me as if I were some nuisance when I made my request.

"*Bhaiyya, mere* earphones *gir gaye*, baggage belt *ke paas. Andar jaaon*? Please," I pleaded.

He didn't say a word. Shit! Does he not understand my Hindi? I tried some English. The reaction was stonier than before. He stood firm and resolute. Bloodied but unbowed. I contemplated bidding a mental, silent goodbye to those damn lost earphones, and order a new pair the next morning. As I stood confused, from the corner of my eye, I saw Vivek walking towards the gate. Oh or was it me? He had a particularly annoying smirk on his face. Now what did this bugger want?

"Another mess, Oinks? What have you gotten into this time?" In the past, when I was young and carefree and idiotic, I had gotten into quite a few situations. Back in those days, Vivek had bailed me out of all those. Regularly. Old habits die hard. I was again sorely tempted to ask him to help. Better sense prevailed.

"Have you still not learned to mind your business? Why are you here?"

"You weren't there. I wanted to say goodbye to you. They told me you are here."

"Huh, what?!" Vivek chuckled and pulled me into a hug, even before I could blink my eyes. *What is going on*? "Look, what are you doing?" I hissed, breaking free. He smiled, rather fondly. "Ok, that was uncalled for. I apologise. But you looked so cute, couldn't resist. I came here to give you these. You had dropped it near the baggage belt. Looking for these, *na*?"

My earphones. I was so happy to see them that it was my turn to behave uncharacteristically. "Thank you so, so much!" I squeezed his hand and beamed at him. He smiled at me. That crinkly smile and I had butterflies in my stomach. I was in love. Again. With the same guy who had dumped me years ago ... for my best friend!

12

I woke up the next morning, surprisingly, early and fresh. Not at all grumpy. Strange. The bed at Rosewood Hotel felt fluffy and soft. Hmm, nice, I lolled around a bit more. And then I remembered. *Fuck. fuck. fuck. All for a pair of bloody earphones – which you, idiot, could have easily replaced! Why on earth did you have to go and bloody coo to Vivek?*

The phone beeped. Loudly. Putting a break to my embarrassing thoughts. Hawkeye! Trust him to come to the rescue.

Meeting at DC's office at 10:30 a.m. Let's meet at the lobby at 10:15 a.m. Be there on time.

Wow. It was only 7 a.m. – which gave me a whole lot of time to loll in bed. But I decided not to. Lolling in bed meant confronting those uncomfortable, mortifying thoughts. Instead, a good workout at the gym would banish these thoughts. Enthused by my own enthusiasm (rare, if you may), I headed straight to the lobby on my floor only to find a super-hot Vivek, showing off his worked-out muscular self. Fuck. Before I could beat a hasty retreat, he had turned and spotted me. Beaming that toe-curling, breath-taking, heart-stopping smile, he walked towards me.

Shit! When on earth did he become so charming? Even my non-objective, obsessed, idiotic heart knew clearly well that it wasn't the case way back then. But time had worked its wonders on this man.

"Oinks, up so early? How come? The meeting is at 10:30. Going to the gym?" He asked, looking me up and down, as I continued to gawk.

Shut your gaping mouth and answer – you idiot.

"Uh hmmm, yes," I mumbled as the elevator door opened.

"Didn't know you work out. But then, there seems to be much about you that I don't know. I am sorry, Oinks. I do not know what happened that you got so mad at me back then in school. Look, I know you are still mad at me, but can we please be at least cordial with each other now? We have to work together for the next couple of months."

Huh, Vivek was apologising? Claiming that he didn't know what happened? And all because he had a face to save. Bloody maintain 'cordial relations' and keep up appearances? I felt the old hurt and anger well up within me. But before I could blurt out a word, the elevator door opened on to the 9th floor in front of the gym. There, Ishita was standing, bright, and chirpy, glowing and blinding in that ghastly golden yellow t-shirt and gym pants.

"Vivek, that took you so long. Forever, only. Oh hello, Oin … Oindrilla, right? Nice to meet you again."

"Have you been waiting for a while, Ishita?" Vivek beamed – now at that tall, svelte lady. Ever so typically, the anger converted into tears and threatened to come out of my eyes.

Blinking my eyes hard, and refusing to make a fool of myself, I smiled, mumbled something and walked into the gym. The blasted earphones, yes, the same ones that Vivek had rescued the previous night, came to my rescue. Blocking any external noises – Ishita's chirping – more like it, I focussed on the loud song blaring in my ears, and the treadmill. Of course, I was still pissed – firstly Vivek claimed that he didn't know what he had done! My bloody foot! And then he was cooing at this Ishita. *Jeez, Oindrilla, you loser, you are jealous. Get a grip!*

Anger has a great effect on one's workout. The gym session turned out to be great. I ignored the man, even though he tried twice to say something to me, and went back for a quick shower and breakfast. And I reached the lobby even before Hawkeye could. Yay. Oindrilla Roy was going to be the most professional as she dealt with the government of Shillong and worked on life-altering government interventions. I was truly set for the day.

And then my phone beeped. It was Ma.

Ma: Where is Ankita?

Me: Huh? I am in Shillong, how would I know?

Radio silence. Ma was totally bonkers! Why on earth would she ask me about Ankita's whereabouts? I parked these thoughts, as I spotted Aparna (please note – I have stopped calling her NBA; she was rather nice) and Hawkeye walking towards me.

I beamed them a huge smile – Hawkeye and Aparna – NOT the annoying people behind me. Aparna did a slight double-take. Naturally, it was rather OOC (out of character) of me to go beaming at Hawkeye and NBA ... no, Aparna. But what the heck. If I had to work here, I might as well be cordial and nice. I couldn't afford to have too many antagonistic people around me. *Brilliant Oinks, you are finally behaving like an adult.*

Once pleasantries were exchanged, we set off to the DC's office, where we were supposed to meet the Additional Deputy

Commissioner before commencing the three-month long project while being stationed at the Child Development Project Office (CDPO).

Suddenly I was excited – again. You see, I was indeed a workaholic. Or as Divya, once snidely put it (with sniggers and all) – "Oh Oinks, you are such a school girl at heart!" A Friday night that was. We were at a pub in Cyber Hub (where else!) and I was all set to guzzle down some bottles of beer and drown my work-related frustration when Hawkeye called. I scooted back to the office – getting drunk and plans of drowning in alcohol were completely forgotten, instead I drowned myself in work.

Coming back to the point of this unnecessary digression. Ever since the jerk had re-entered my life, I needed something to distract myself – and the only new thing in my professional life was this project. And what else was I to do to get my mind off him – other than work? Hence, the excitement.

But life had other plans and so it was in this case as well. My phone beeped – urgently, frantically, maniacally, when we were listening to the Deputy Commissioner (*God bless him, he was the same one who had given that Vinay character the boot!)* pontificate on the benefits of this project we were about to embark on. Sensible and wise he may have been, he was also however rather ancient – and had a rather languorous way of speaking. His soft voice, slow speech, were a perfect remedy for insomniacs. It could put anyone to sleep. And at that moment, as I pretended to be attentive, my phone started beeping. Thankfully, it was on silent and only I could feel the vibrations, as the flurry of messages came in.

Wrong. Hawkeye, sitting next to me, was looking at me with a particularly supercilious smile on his face. Pointing to my phone, he sniggered, in a whisper of course, "Oindrilla, your phone. Can you go out and switch it off, please?"

Shit. Nodding and looking probably like a dying duck, I stepped out of the plush Additional DC's office and whipped that annoying device out. 50 UNREAD MESSAGES?

Out of which nearly 46 of them were from Ma! Seriously?! What the bloody heck was going on?

"Rolling your eyes again, Oinks. What's up?"

I looked up to see Vivek walking out of the room. He had his phone in his hand, and a smirk plastered on his face.

"What are you doing here?" I questioned.

He looked surprised at first and then chuckled, "Oinks, I love you, as always. But no, I am not following you." There was a hint of seriousness that crept in his voice and eyes (oh those damn, mesmerising brown eyes) and I felt a shiver literally run down my spine – the good kind of shiver.

OINDRILLA ROY. YOU MORON. CHECK YOUR MESSAGES.

Glaring at Vivek, but not really retorting back, I peeked into those 50 odd messages that Ma had sent. It had not even been a day since I last saw her.

Ma: Where is Ankita?

Ma: Has she told you?

Ma: Do you know?

Ma: Mamu and Mami very upset. Call them. Where is Ankita?

How the hell was I supposed to know where Ankita was? But where was she? And then it struck me. Had that idiot cousin of mine eloped with her lover boy? Oh shit.

I called Ma, who picked up immediately. "Tinku, Ankita *kothai*? She is nowhere to be found. Her phone is switched off. Do you have any clue?"

"Ma, I don't. She said she would call me yesterday but she never did."

"OK. I have a meeting. Think about where she could have gone."

What the hell!

"Are you ok?" Vivek was asking me, with concern writ large in his eyes, as he stood rather too close for my own comfort.

"Yes, I am ok," I said, attempting to step back. And then just like that, because I couldn't keep it any longer in my stomach, I added, "Ankita is nowhere to be found. I think she has run away from home."

"What? When? Ankita?"

"That's what my mom told me just now."

"That doesn't really seem right. She seemed too sensible to be running away from home, Oinks. You are more the type," he smirked.

I let the jibe pass. I was way too distraught to think straight. "Well, I am going inside. I will think about this mess later," I said before moving past Vivek to walk into the room.

The rest of the meeting as well as the day passed off in a daze. I wasn't paying that much attention – just perfunctory enough to not make an ass of myself.

Not that much happened. The Deputy Commissioner welcomed us all, and detailed his view of what this project should achieve (typical top *sarkari* hyperbolic bull shit!). Following this, which Hawkeye enthusiastically preened and made a *lamba-chauda* presentation (the one that I had worked on in Kolkata as I waited for that Ankita who-now-was-nowhere-to-be-found to come back). What a nonsense presentation this was. Not the PPT (that was top class, if I may say so; I used Prezi!) but the way Hawkeye screeched and delivered it – in that irritatingly high-pitched nasal tone. That was super annoying!

I looked around to see if I was the only one getting irritated. And no apparently, I wasn't!

Aparna, who was seated opposite me, was looking distracted too. She caught my eye, smiled a small smile, and bent down.

My phone beeped.

Aparna: Oindrilla, next time Hawk or whatever you call him tells you to make a presentation, please keep it short… ;)

LMAO.

Me: Noted ☻

After somnambulating through the remaining presentation, Hawkeye was finally done. Next steps were firmed up, asses of the higher-ups conveniently licked, this torture eventually came to an end. To me, another one was to begin. Though it was expected anyway from the moment I knew I would be working with the jerk, Vivek and that sexy Ishita.

OK broad picture explanation time. Among the many fuck-all activities that EOFA was involved in, one of them was what we call 'technological interventions to benefit the life of the needy and underprivileged'.

Don't get fooled by this baloney and jargon. What it meant in simple terms was this – EOFA had bullied some *bechara* tech start-up guy to part with his application/software. Post this bullying and sort of takeover of application, EOFA had also managed to find some *bechara* (ok not so *bechara* in this case) client who was willing to part with an arm and a leg to implement the said application in their set-up. And I was now supposed to be here, along with *bechara* tech start-up guy (dishy, sweet Rajat, who should be landing up in

Shillong sometime soon) to make sure that the product was implemented.

Now, where do Vivek and Ishita come in?

In this case, the *bechara* client, which is not so *bechara,* was a cash-strapped government department. And these *sarkari* and public sector fellows were majorly enamoured with the Big 4 consulting firms. For some reason, they believed that these Big 4 guys were magicians—in reality, they were high-priced, suit-boot-wearing consultants spouting jargon from Harvard Business Review. And these magicians with their bloody wands could cure all ills plaguing the government, the nation and the world. Hence, they had parted with their big bucks to one of these Big 4 for most of these 'transformation' projects. And that is when they realised – these magicians knew bugger-all but to spout fancy words. Then the government department *wallahs* started looking for actual technology and this was where EOFA came in – pimping innocent tech start-ups (who had skills/ technology but no connections) and getting its cut!

Phew. Vivek and Ishita were apparently in what is called the Project Management Unit (PMU) here – they would manage the whole project. Rajat, who developed this great software, would be there to help with the technical implementation of it. And me? What was I doing here? Well, I was to work in-between with both Rajat and Vivek. *Wah*! What a nice way to describe my work.

13

The moment that boring-to-death presentation finally ended in the DC's office, Hawkeye stopped me. Aparna was also with him. *Aargh. Fuck it. Might as well distract myself with work before trying to figure out what was on back in Cal!*

"Oindrilla, *ab tum iss* Vivek *se apni* setting *kar lo acchi*?"

"HUH?? What?" I gape, looking at Hawkeye. What the fuck was he blabbering about? Oh shit, he meant that I should have a good *working* relationship with Vivek. *OINDRILLA ROY, get your mind out of the gutter.*

Hawkeye looked at me strangely, "*Theek ho*?"

I gawked further. Hawkeye oscillated between being downright annoying to suddenly caring. These sudden oscillations meant that one never knew which Hawkeye one was talking to at the moment. However, I was genuinely touched by his sudden concern and decided to be upfront.

"That was Ma. *Haan*, problem at home. I will sort that later, Rahul. Will go and meet Vivek and Ishita."

"Ok. Ishita is leaving tonight. Your main point of contact will be Vivek. You should get to know him. He is here somewhere."

OMG. Get to know him indeed. To think that is all I wanted to do once upon a time. *And that too in the Biblical sense. OINDRILLA – look up from the gutter, you moron.*

I nodded as demurely as I could and excused myself. Just then Vivek, who was lurking somewhere there anyway, made an appearance, beaming and all.

"Hello, Rahul. This is Vivek. Hello, Oin … Oind … Oindrilla. Sorry, I hope that's your name. Hello Aparna."

The bugger was oozing so much bloody charm that both Hawkeye and NBA were floored. Oin/Oind/Oindrilla, indeed. *Bastard.*

"Hello Vivek, I am looking forward to working with you," I cooed back, all smiles, and fluttering eyelashes. "Oh, where is Ishita?" I pretended to look around. Just at that moment, Hawkeye got a call. It was the Boss. And Aparna got busy with some official from the DC's office. Thank God, Vivek and I were spared this drama of being extra polite and civil with each other. But the jerk had other ideas.

"Where are we meeting, Oinks? I thought you wanted to get to know me better. Should we just head back to the hotel?" Vivek said seriously, before breaking into a big smile upon seeing my horrified, dying-duck expression.

"Shut up, Vivek. Why are we even meeting today? Why don't we catch up tomorrow morning when Rajat will be here?" I retorted. I was now beginning to get unnecessarily worked up.

Vivek surprised me by replying gently, "Why don't you just call home and find out about Ankita? I am here only. Will catch hold of some of these people here. And then when you are ready, we could head to the CDPO office."

I nodded, headed to a corner and pulled out my phone. 50 WhatsApp messages! 13 SMSes and 5 missed calls. *Holy shit. Now what the fuck is going on?* Out of the 50 WA messages; 30 were from Ma, 5 from Mami, 3 from Mamu and 12 from Sweety. Thank God for Sweety. I badly needed to speak to her. But that was for later. First things first. Where was Ankita? What had she done? Or what had that lover boy Prabhas done? Suddenly I was nervous. She had been looking rather lost and worried when I last saw her. What if he had jilted her? Left her holding the baby? And what if Ankita had jumped off the Howrah Bridge, unable to face Mamu, Mami, and Dida? (Aargh, I wish she had told me. I would have taught her to be like those brave K-drama girls – fighting to survive. To become a single, cool mum.) *Oindrilla – stop speculating and read those messages.*

Muttering curses and all sorts of silent obscenities at the lover boy, Prabhas, I read those 38 messages!

Well, that nutcase cousin of mine had eloped with her lover boy, having left note and all. Where to? Well, everyone at home thought I had helped her. Not just helped her but actually masterminded the whole elopement. Facepalm. Shit. I spent the next 15 minutes, talking to everyone and convincing them that I had NOTHING to do with Ankita's elopement. I didn't even know who this fucking Prabhas was. *Shotti.* Convinced or not, I got away at last, citing that I had a meeting to attend. Which was partially true. Wasn't Vivek lurking around somewhere waiting for me to finish sorting out this mess? I cut the call and looked around. There he was at a distance, leaning against the wall, conversing attentively with one of the government officials. Laughing. With that smile, those dimples lighting up his face. I was suddenly breathless. Bloody, it was as if I had been punched in my heart, stomach, gut, liver and whichever part is the seat of passion. *Oindrilla ROY, have some sense. Stop melting into a puddle – at least pick someone else, if you have to. Not the same guy – even after these many years. If you can't get a grip, go bang your head against a wall.*

Sweety! Where are you? I remembered her, out of a sheer sense of desperation and habit (you see, I need some sense knocked into my pathetic head immediately). Oh fuck. She had messaged as well.

S: Oinks, help! help! help!

S: Oinks, where are you? Need to talk, girl.

S: OINDRILLA ROY YOU DON'T ANSWER MY CALLS. YOU DON'T REPLY TO MY MESSAGES EITHER.

S: Ok, I get it. You must be in a meeting. WHENEVER you see these fuck-all messages, you better fucking call me.

OMFG. Now what had gone wrong there? Seriously. Maybe as Tejas suggested to me a few weeks back, I should go and meet that Priya Devi lady. Digression time folks. A few weeks back, in my *tatti jeevan*, lots of *tatti* things had happened to me. Some major trouble at work, thanks to NBA and OBA and also an accident. So, one evening, some weeks back, there was this *maha* crazy deadline that Tejas and I were chasing. Some documents had to be submitted, for which we required a few inputs from this business manager called Tejinder. He was one shrewd guy – also played politics till we figured. He kept giving us *golis* but wouldn't give us the necessary information. I had had enough and was hell-bent on retrieving the inputs from him. I chased him and stood in front of his cubicle, trying to get his attention. That bugger was on the phone, singing sweet nothings to his pretty wife or girlfriend or someone. Within the 5 minutes that I left my workstation (which was in front of his) in order to take an overdue bathroom break, the bugger had packed his bags and already left! I chased him, undeterred, down the stairs. And that's when I lost my footing and fell down with a thud ... one straight floor below – shrieking and screaming. He finally stopped coochie-cooing on the phone and took notice of me! The idiot that I was, even in that pained state, asked him the few questions I had been itching to get answers to. Yay!

Tejas thought I was mad. No, he told me so when he was driving me back home from the hospital – the OPD wing of a major hospital was located, luckily for me, on the ground floor of my office building. I had been told that I had fractured my fucking tailbone. As I rattled off the crucial bits of inputs required for the project delivery with supreme glee, despite excruciating pain, Tejas shook his head disapprovingly and told me that I was stark, raving nuts. And then he mentioned Priya Devi – an astrologer famous in Gurgaon apparently. Whom he had visited. "*Tera* time *kharab chal raha hai,* Oinks. *Tu iss aurat se jaake mil.*"

I stared at him; spell bound. Was this my buddy? My smart, sensible Tejas? He believed in this mumbo-jumbo. "*Hein*, Tejas? I fell on my bum. Broke it. So bloody what? And time *toh us din se kharaab chal raha hai jab se* I joined EOFA. Big shit, man!" Tejas, the sweet guy, persisted. His mum, who was a part of some married women FB group, consulted with Priya Devi ji. Priya Devi ji never got anything wrong. Her predictions were accurate. Why, she even told Tejas' mum when to speak and when to shut up, when to step out and when to eat!

I remembered Priya Devi ji right now. I suddenly wanted to meet her. My cousin had run away. My bestie who had turned out to be a lesbian was sending me panicky messages. And I was turning into a puddle every time the one and only guy who I fell in love with years ago came back in my line of sight. And I had to work with him for three months. Wouldn't have been a problem, had he fallen in love with me back then. But he hadn't. He had fallen in love with my then best friend Shreya instead.

Composing myself, I called Sweety. I had to find out what had made her this frantic. And soon wished I had never called. Sweety and Divya had eloped and they were headed to Shillong. To meet me. And rope me in to convince uncle and aunty. FUCK MY LIFE.

Two elopements. Both of which had nothing to do with me. In one, the fam already held me complicit. In the other, I was soon to become complicit, by virtue of being in Shillong.

"Oinks. Are you ok?" I suppose I must have looked very lost. Vivek was now in front of me, flying hair, dimpled smile and all. I hadn't noticed.

I nodded. "Let's go then. Whom are we meeting first? How do we go about on this project?" I tried, to restore a sense of normalcy and professionalism, in my head, that is.

Vivek didn't say a word. He looked at me seriously, and then led me by the arm towards the office cab that was waiting by the gate.

"Let us get back to the hotel first." As I sat inside, wordlessly, still in a state of complete shock, he added gently, "What's the matter, Oinks? All well at home? Any news of Ankita?"

"She has run away. With whom I don't know and where I don't know. They think I had something to do with this," I barked, terribly annoyed and irritated.

"What?" Vivek looked zapped. "Who? They being aunty and Ankita's family?"

"Not so much Mamu and Mami but Ma. My own mother. According to Ma, Ankita is so sweet, so sensible and oh so docile. Aargh. Makes me want to puke. Unlike me. If such a paragon of virtue has run away from home, especially a day after meeting me, then obviously I had something to do with it, no?" I snapped. Though why was I taking it out on him I knew not.

Vivek was being an absolute darling. He was listening to me, attentively, gentleness and concern reflecting in his deep dark eyes. I looked into his eyes and was about to drown in them (*you idiot – stop thinking of romance*) when the phone rang.

"Ankitaaaaaaaaaaaaaaaaaa!" I yelled into the phone. It got cut.

"That was Ankita," I said.

"I heard that. I am not deaf. Why, that *chai wala* uncle also heard you," smirked Vivek, pointing to a man who owned a small tea shop in a shack by the road.

I smacked him on his arm without giving it much thought. Not that it stopped him from laughing. He continued to do so. Thankfully for me, the Rosewood Hotel came into sight and I was spared of any snarky response that my thoughtless action would have normally elicited.

14

"Now that we are here, and we still have not spent even ten minutes discussing the project, why don't we head to the café and grab a cup of coffee?" Vivek suggested as we alighted from the cab at Rosewood Hotel.

I nodded, quite shamefacedly. You see I had completely forgotten about the goddamn implementation and project, how irresponsible. But work was the last thing on my mind that afternoon. My mind was stuck in Delhi and Cal; going over and over those bizarre events like a broken tape recorder. Why on earth would my closest (and only) cousin and my bestest friend choose the same fucking day to elope? Not with each other. But with their respective loves of their lives? Why on earth would they then indict me and bring me into the picture? The cousin, unknowingly – Ankita had not blamed me for any of her shenanigans. But Sweety had. She told me that in her note which would reach her parents later tonight, she clearly mentioned that if I was aware and could be supportive of her true love (for Divya), why oh why couldn't they be?

Now that I gave my conversation with Sweety a deeper thought, this whole bit struck me as a tad bit unfair. What did she mean? Was I that prudish? Was I a homophobe? Was I such a stick in the mud? Geez. Since both my bestie and cousin were not near me, I decided to check with the one person in front of me.

"Am I a homophobe? Do I come across like that?"

We were seated at the café in Rosewood Hotel and Vivek was stuffing his mouth with a chocolate croissant. Upon being asked this sudden question from nowhere, he choked and sputtered. "WHAT?" Before breaking into a round of coughs. When the coughing and choking had subsided, he started looking around everywhere.

"*Hein*, how weird can you be! Stop being so conscious. Everyone coughs. It is okay," I patted his arm.

"Oinks, are you out of your head? I was checking to see whom you were looking at."

"Whom would I look at? I wasn't looking at anyone. Why? Is there someone there whom we know? Or whom I need to look at?" My turn to stare at him and look around with a gaping mouth.

"You duffer. Didn't you ask me a question just now? I am looking to see if there are any gay/lesbian couples around – which prompted your question," Vivek hissed, in a loud whisper.

"Ah that. No no, the question was prompted by something else. I have been accused of being a homophobe."

"By whom?"

"My best friend."

Vivek stopped stuffing his mouth and stared at me. "And what did you do that prompted such a grave accusation. Are you a homophobe?"

"No. I am not. Well, she didn't really accuse me. I think she implied it."

"You think? Seriously, Oinks?" He shook his head and started chuckling. "Haven't changed a bit, have you? Still presumptuous. Assuming things that never existed thanks to the havoc created mainly inside your idle mind."

I was furious. Whatever did he mean? Who did he think he was, to pronounce judgements on me, when he clearly doesn't know a thing! But before I could bark out an adequate reply and put the conceited bugger back in his place, guess who made an appearance.

Dear old Hawkeye.

"Oindrilllaaaaaa! You are here! Hello Vivek, good to see you both clearing all doubts about this implementation. Whatever Vinay had done or not done, we need to make sure that the implementation is top-notch and goes off according to budget and plan." He came and plonked himself on the chair next to us.

Pulling on the straightest face that I could, I nodded. Vivek was better. He smiled, *oh that charming smile of his*, and said glibly, "We are sorting out all areas which could become a matter of conflict before we head into the project with full gusto starting tomorrow, Rahul. Who at the CDPO do we need to meet tomorrow to get a more detailed view?"

Hawkeye beamed, a most paternal smile, and for a minute I thought he was going to pat me on my head. A smile which suddenly made me even more forlorn as I missed Baba. *Good Lord! I must be officially losing it completely. Hawkeye and Baba? In front of Vivek.* Who was the ultimate and original problem. The other problems being the untraceable Ankita and the unstoppable Sweety and Divya, who would be here the very next day or the day after that or well, some day in the near future.

"Oindrilla, when is Rajat landing?"

"Rajat should have been here by now. He had sent me his flight details. Let me check," I looked at my phone, suddenly feeling lighter. Rajat Bhat, the hot dude, sweet guy, tech genius, entrepreneur who has somehow gotten trapped in the clutches of EOFA. Good for us! Good for me. You see, other than Tejas, who was my work-spouse literally, if there was one friend I had in my working life, it was this guy – Rajat.

Rajat and I had hit it off instantly when we met last year on yet another implementation in Mahbubnagar, Telangana. We spent more than two months there – with Rajat flying in and out of Hyderabad while Tejas and I were permanently stuck. Sick of the hotel accommodation, Tejas and I had even rented a small flat – much to the chagrin of the locals, who couldn't digest the fact that a young man and woman were flatmates! Add to that Rajat who would become the third flatmate, each time he was in town. Boy, my reputation in that small colony in Mahbubnagar was completely in tatters. But because people there were generally nice – they just bitched and gossiped – I was fine. No shady advances made, because my morals were perceived to be lax and found fucking wanting!

Coming back to Rajat, thinking of his pleasant, chiselled face brightened up my mood. I checked upon his flight schedule and squealed excitedly, "Ooh he should have been here by now." Vivek looked up, sharply, with a raised eyebrow. Considering I was close to either breaking someone's head or bursting into a volley of angry tears a few minutes earlier, this exuberance on my part must have seemed strange. He probably was convinced I was either mad or crazy.

"*Arre haan*, I forgot, you are good friends, *na*. One of Oindrilla's close friends. Which is why she looks so happy," interjected Hawkeye, in a paternal nasal tone, with an equally warm, pathetic paternal look in his eyes. Fuck. He must be missing his daughters. He should go back. That was the problem with these *buddha-buddhi log*. Take them away from their *baccha* party, they start viewing anyone younger than them as being *bacchas*. Even Aparna, formerly bitchily referred by me as NBA, was treating me like a *baccha* – keeping an eye over me. Why, she had messaged me half an hour back asking if I was okay. She had noticed that I was looking tense. Of course, I hadn't replied to her message; I was busy venting to Vivek, who now had a frown on his face. What brought about this frown I know not. Guess, the conscientious bugger (*well, he was that way back then too*) must have been worrying about the time that he had whiled away and wasted so far that particular day. But before I could ask him, Hawkeye waved and said, "Oh look, Rajat and Aparna are headed this way!"

Oh Rajat Bhat. How much I missed him, I realised then. The past two days had been tough – coping with the shock of seeing Vivek again, the news of the two elopements (and my role, or not, in them) and my own jumbled up mind and heart with its *hazaar* and one complicated thoughts and emotions, I sorely needed a friend. Why, had the shitty day continued this way, I would have called Tejas and asked him to come to Shillong. And informed Hawkeye and Aparna that I couldn't work in such a hostile environment alone. Their reactions, I well could have imagined. Hostile? The environment was certainly not hostile. Beautiful, picturesque Shillong – with all its natural charm and lush greenery in plain, fucking sight – could not be termed hostile. Vivek, who may have been hostile to me, because he was a jerk who broke my heart (which these two people did not know about), was also being rather nice. Too nice. That was the whole bloody problem. How could I tell them that? If I kept hanging out with him, and if he sat around, listening to my sob stories so nicely and sweetly and caringly, I would fall in love with him. Again. And he wouldn't fall in love with me. Again.

OINDRILLA ROY, you are in love already. You never stopped being in love. Stop sounding like a deluded idiot.

Oh Rajat – it was so good to see him.

In that absolutely ecstatic state, I waved to Rajat grinning and extremely enthusiastic, prompting Hawkeye to continue in that fucking, and annoying paternal tone. "*Arre*, *wah*, at least someone brings such a big smile to your face. Good, I was beginning to get worried that I shouldn't have proposed your name for this outstation project."

"Oh, Rajat is a dear friend. I am seriously happy to see him," I replied cheerfully. Even that nasal twang of Hawkeye was not bothering me at that moment. Rajat was the one ray of hope in my *tatti-bhara jeevan*.

"Rajat is a good guy," averred Hawkeye, a smile on his face, also paternal, as he agreed with me.

If Hawkeye was smiling, then God knows what went wrong with Vivek. There was a dark cloud on his till then cheerful face. Almost as if he had indigestion. Well, he wolfed down three – not one – chocolate croissants. *Please note, I counted because I wanted to eat them. But I desisted as I was agitated and I have a history of eating when upset and gaining 10 kilos in a day. Ok that's a fucking exaggeration. But you get what I am getting at.* And anyone who ate three croissants, huge ones at that, without even offering it to the upset person sitting in front of them, deserved to get indigestion. And he must have. Forgetting whatever little tact I possessed, and speaking without thinking, as I always did, I asked him, "Vivek, you have a stomach ache?"

A frown appeared in the midst of that dark cloud. "Do I? Why do you ask?"

"You ate 3 huge chocolate croissants and now you are frowning. Hence..."

He frowned a bit more and didn't say a word.

"*Arre,* Oindrillaa ... you are counting the number of croissants he ate. *Chee chee, aise* count *nahin karte. Tumhare liye mangaoon*?" Hawkeye butted in.

I was tempted. Should I say yes? They looked very good. But then Rajat and Aparna made an appearance at the table. And I forgot. About the croissants.

"Rajatttt, how are you?" I said, giving him a warm, warm hug. Rajat was also chuffed to see me. He beamed and said, "Good, ya. Why didn't you call me back? I called you earlier from the airport."

Oh fuck. One of those missed calls was from him.

"Oh so sorry. I didn't check my phone," I apologised. He smiled as he sat down at the table. And paternal Hawkeye launched into a quick round of introductions. Since only Rajat and Vivek didn't know each other, they were introduced to one another. Poor Vivek must be really having a bad case of indigestion. He was smiling at Rajat, but it was such a perfunctory smile. Not the charming, warm, crinkly one that made my toes curl. The full charm was not to be unleashed on him. A conversation began about all and sundry and as it progressed, I felt happy. Just looking at the chiselled perfection that Rajat Bhat was. Thank God for the distraction. Anything to avoid staring at Vivek Rao, whose indigestion certainly wasn't getting better. Five minutes later he excused himself, gave me a rather strange, curt look, bade the others a polite goodbye and left for his room. Strange. The desperate, idiotic, hopeless self that I was, I felt forlorn. If I am to admit to myself, it had indeed been great to be with him the entire morning. Luckily, I was spared more frank and disconcerting internal admissions to myself. What with Hawkeye, Aparna and Rajat around me on the table. It was inevitable that we chalked out a rather defining plan for the implementation of the software in the selected *anganwadis*.

OK. More work related context. EOFA, with its *dhansoo* government connects, all thanks to the Big Boss who was one kick-ass IAS officer in his pre-EOFA days, had managed to convince the Deputy Commissioner of East Khasi Hills that there was this technical innovation that would solve all ills and magically transform all *anganwadis* under the CDPO into a futuristic day-care centre, where kids get milk and honey and bla di bla. You get the drift.

Now the Deputy Commissioner, the same venerable gentleman whose drone we were subjected to this morning, and the one whose only good deed as far as I was concerned was sacking Vinay the creep, happened to be an old friend of the Big Boss. And also my parents. They were all from the same Civil Services batch you see. So, for the sake of old times, and good old camaraderie, EOFA had snagged the contract and we arm twisted Rajat Bhat, the entrepreneur whose baby this innovation was, promising him some great returns, into coming here to Shillong to install and implement it.

Now what hold EOFA had on Rajat Bhat, I do not know. I was almost let in on the big secret one evening in Mahbubnagar, when we got drunk in a snazzy, glitzy pub. Wait, there were no pubs – snazzy or tacky anywhere in Mahbubnagar. Let me rephrase. It was during our Mahbubnagar project. It was such a dead, hole-in-the-wall kind a place. With nothing to do, we would often go to Hyderabad to basically do something, anything over the weekends. It was on one such outing that at a snazzy pub, we both got so drunk and Rajat had started blurting out – about EOFA, his meeting with the Big Boss, how he got snared and how now he wanted out. Oh, in that drunk state, he also started saying something about how I was the one bright spot in Mahbubnagar, or was it EOFA? But before he could complete that, Tejas puked all over the place. So, we had to pay up and drag ourselves back home. No, no drunk driving – we had an office car at our disposal, all days of the week. That way, EOFA and also Hawkeye were rather considerate.

Then that was it. What hold EOFA had on Rajat Bhat – I still didn't know. I decided that moment that since we both would be stuck touring picturesque East Khasi Hill district for a while (what a change this was from the dry, arid and stinky Mahbubnagar), that I would get him to tell all the shady secrets of the Big Boss and EOFA. Not that I was keenly interested in any of those secrets. It was because I did not want to spend my time pining and mooning over Vivek Rao and I certainly did not want to display my pathetic self in front of him anymore. Rajat Bhat was therefore a nice and a safe distraction.

15

Coming back to that evening; we landed up having a productive outing. Plans were made and finalised for the next day. It was decided that all of us, including Vivek, would go meet the officials at the CDPO office at 10 a.m. the next day; post which we would go visiting the shortlisted *anganwadis*, which would act as the first *bakras* for the test pilot.

The Deputy Commissioner was also not such a fool who would bite into anything his friend (EOFA's Big Boss) would try palming off. He had agreed for a test pilot implementation to begin with. And before we landed here, Tejas and I had done a virtual study of all the *anganwadis* in his district and had shortlisted a few. This list had been passed on to Hawkeye and the Big Boss to vet and bless. Of course, since Hawkeye never bothered looking at it and the Big Boss (after years of note making) was more interested in spelling mistakes and turn of phrases only, the list was final!

Imagine, we had spent the whole evening deciding these two seemingly simple things. But no, it hardly felt that way. To my shocked surprise (could surprise be a shock? Didn't this sound rather oxymoronish? OH MY FUCKING GOD,

Oindrilla, you have become a minor Big Boss – focussing on words and language, shut up), the late afternoon/evening discussion at the café in Rosewood Hotel turned out to be fun.

Hawkeye, in the days before he became my boss, and was a mere colleague, used to be so much fun. The old Hawkeye made a belated appearance that day; perhaps because we were not in our fuck-all office, dealing with those familiar fuck-all tensions. Or maybe we were in Shillong – such a beautiful place; even though this didn't quite hold. We were seated all evening in a plush restaurant/café inside Rosewood Hotel, so some fucking Shillong we saw. Anyway, the crux of the matter was that it was great. Contrary to my views on Aparna (erstwhile NBA as I thought of her), she turned out to be a sweetheart. Funny, thoughtful and warm, she was the surprise of that trip – other than Vivek, who by the by had made an appearance back right in time for dinner. Actually, when we were about to have dinner, I wondered, not loudly, definitely not, as to what Vivek was upto. It didn't seem right for us to eat without him, or so I thought. (*Bah bah* what a crap load of shit. Felt – not thought! Admit it, you pathetic girl, you were missing him and wanted to see him again. Don't credit yourself for being that thoughtful or generous otherwise!)

Now, Aparna turned out to be truly thoughtful amongst us. She remembered Vivek. "*Accha*, Rahul, what about the PWC guy? Vivek? Shouldn't we call him? *Bechara*, else he will have to eat alone."

Hawkeye heartily agreed with this suggestion. So it was, Vivek joined us in the next 10 minutes, as we headed out for dinner. "Hey, Vivek, good you could make it. Has Ishita left?" That was Hawkeye at his welcoming best. "Thanks. She did. You guys had a productive afternoon?" I heard Vivek ask. I was of course not looking at Vivek. Instead, I was peering into Rajat's phone where he was showing Aparna and me some silly memes. Aparna, being the well-mannered, good-intentioned, mummy type, looked up and greeted Vivek, "Hey guys, Vivek is here. We should eat now." It was more of a reprimand to remind us to be civil. Which Rajat was. I merely stared at Vivek, sullenly, and nodded. Vivek on his part didn't say anything either. The dark *indigestion-wala* cloud was back on his face – or perhaps, it had never left. Had I been the Oindrilla Roy of the past, meaning the senseless twelfth standard girl, I would have gone over and asked him what the matter was. But I was now grown up and mature. Hence despite curiosity gnawing at my insides, I didn't say a word.

***

Dinner was rather a subdued affair. I simply didn't want to talk. I was tongue-tied. Seeing Vivek again after a gap of hold-your-breath three hours (!!) suddenly made me feel like going and hugging him. Also, he was looking rather grumpy himself. I wanted to ruffle his hair, smooth his brow and kiss his worries away. *Sheesh*. Of course, it (even the hug) would have been misconstrued – no, not by Vivek (he would have simply raised his eyebrow and smirked). But the others, who were blissfully unaware of our history, which I am sure was more magnified in my fucking mind than what it actually was. And then he was looking absolutely brooding, nerdy and dishy. Better than Rajat Bhat, who any way took the cake when it comes to looks – tall, fair, muscular – a typically charming Pahadi-Punjabi guy as compared to the dusky, thin, nerdy looking South Indian Vivek. But to me that moment, Vivek was looking so charming that I was back to my melt-to-a-puddle state. *Oindrilla Jeez.* Anyway, with such jumbled up thoughts, I thought it better to shut up than make an ass of myself.

However, my silence didn't go unnoticed. When I went to get myself a second helping of the dessert, my favourite *rosogulla*, I bumped into Aparna. She was also standing and staring at those white beauties with such love. "I love *rosogullas*. So big and juicy." *Gosh, why was she sounding orgasmic? No, she didn't sound that bad. You have a bloody gutter mind.* Then she added, "Are you feeling well? You have been rather silent through the dinner." I smiled, a forced smile, "Yes, all well. You know me, I am not the friendliest of people. Today has been rather hectic. Plus, I spoke so much during our planning session. Want to hit the bed early." An answer which she was satisfied with, for she continued to ogle at the dessert section – with renewed focus.

"Oh, by the way, we are on for Wednesday, right? The sightseeing plan we made on the flight." Oh shit, I had completely forgotten about that.

"Yes, as of now, definitely. But largely depends on what happens tomorrow. I need to request Hawkeye also," I replied as I waited for her to stop ogling at the dessert and actually fill her plate up.

"Hmm, you know what? I will bring it up now," Aparna said, quickly adding some *hazaar* things on to her plate. It was my turn to ogle at her. "What? Why are you staring, Oindrilla?"

"Don't mind my asking this please. But you have kids, no?" I blurted, still staring at her plate. Aparna guffawed. "Yes, I do. Two brattish boys, aged ten and eight. I think I know why you are asking me this. Why don't you ask me my age directly? Instead of trying to figure out."

Shit. "Sorry, I suffer from a perennial foot-in-mouth syndrome. That was me trying to be tactful."

"That was rather a bad attempt, girl. I turn 40 this year. Yes, yes, I don't look it. I know. Stop gaping and come let's go back." Aparna beamed and indicated that she was done.

I always knew NBA to be older than me, but 40? Boy, she didn't look it one bit. Why I was ogling at her was not for the age thingie – but the fact that she could eat anything and everything, and she does. It doesn't at all show! And here, every sweet I take a bite into, meant 15 extra minutes at the gym. Despite which, I was hogging that day. Because I was really tired – tired of worrying about Ankita; tired about wondering when Sweety and that bitch Divya would land up; and tired of being perennially in love with Vivek, who chose that moment, to show up behind Aparna and me. "Hey, how are the *rosogullas*? Worth trying?" Was he asking me? But he didn't like *rosogullas*. At least I know he didn't back then.

Before I could even register the question, Aparna excitedly replied, "Excellent. You must try them."

He nodded and was about to head towards the counter, when I blurted out, "Since when did you start liking *rosogullas*, Vivek?"

Aparna turned around a bit sharply, "You guys know each other?" After putting foot in mouth, again, I shut up and froze. Thankfully, the charming Vivek came to the rescue. He smiled at me and said, "Since this afternoon." Looking at Aparna, he said, "I was telling her this afternoon at tea that I didn't particularly like *rosogullas*."

"Ah, that way!" Aparna seemed satisfied and started walking towards the table. I was, however, still rooted at the spot. So was Vivek. "You remember? Even now?" I still couldn't speak. I nodded and started walking away towards the table, feeling rather foolish. When Vivek made his appearance again at the table, I noticed that the dark cloud on his face had lifted, just a little.

"Rahul, I have a suggestion. Not entirely work related. But your buy-in and *razamandi* is very much needed. When do you fly back to Delhi?" Aparna said, as we waited for the coffee to be poured.

"Not confirmed yet but it will be either on Thursday or Friday as per the current schedule. Why?"

"Tomorrow, we have the *anganwadi* tour and I suppose, the implementation will begin post that – either Thursday or Friday, as most of these places require at least one day to set up their work space?"

"True…" replied Hawkeye, waiting for Aparna to continue. He had this particularly hawkish expression, thinking, waiting, ready to pounce.

"On Wednesday, why don't we all go sightseeing? Once the work begins in earnest, barring weekends, these three will be stuck either at the *anganwadi* or visiting nearby homes and the hotel. I think, we should look around some places in the city before work actually begins. Of course this shall be on personal expense and we can all take a day off," Aparna elaborated.

Hawkeye continued to think for a bit. Aparna got a call shortly after and she had to excuse herself even before he replied. Vivek was looking at his phone; I was peeking glances at him (which is how I know) and Rajat was staring at me. What the fuck. This was rather strange. The third time during dinner. The first time I was sure, I had something stuck on my face, or in my teeth or something awfully embarrassing like that. But Vivek would have pointed it out – nay, laughed at me – had that been the case. You know, maybe Rajat was just spacing out, looking in my direction. YOU do that often, OINDRILLA ROY! All the time in fact. Really silly (and vain) of me to imagine that he was staring. AT ME. That too.

Phew, finally Aparna was back. "Sorry, sorry. Oh yes, Rahul. What do you think of my suggestion?"

Hawkeye loved these fuck-all situations, where he would be in the spotlight, *baantoing gyaan* and making 'important' decisions! A pity he didn't get these opportunities more often. At EOFA, the Big Boss was the one who makes all decisions – including HR related ones. There was this fuck-all time when the entire building (imagine that too in posh Cyber Hub in ultra-posh and ultra-snooty Gurugram) didn't have water. No water. Even in the bloody loos. And when HR and Admin heads suggested (rather decided) that the employees should go back home, the Big Boss refused! Aargh. Painful it was. The Big Boss called us to the posh conference room, where there was this ultra-hip Nescafe pod ka machine and another tea vending machine and there was a bloody Coffee Day Counter and told us that he had worked in places, of course back in the days when he was *sabka mai-baap*, where there were no toilets. Couldn't we hold our bladders? For just one day? After saying which, he made some fuck-all congratulatory announcement and plied us with doughnuts and coffee.

The point is that at EOFA, it was the Big Boss who decided everything; and at his house, (Rahul's, I mean; not the Big Boss), his wife was the one who called the shots. So poor Hawkeye hardly got such opportunities – and when he got them, he made use of them to the fullest. So, Hawkeye launched into one *lamba*, boring monologue, with only Aparna pretending to listen. I swear, I saw a glazed, bored look in her eyes even.

Vivek, who had stepped out to make a call, was back, and was once again looking at his phone, furiously typing something – texting someone, for sure. But who? And Rajat was AGAIN looking at me.

Since I couldn't ask Rajat, I decided to ask Vivek, not in person but through WhatsApp since Vivek was anyway on his phone. I shot him a message. (Yes, I had his phone number. You see we had been a part of a school alumni WA group the past year. I had saved his number. Even though we didn't speak or chat. Actually, another pathetic confession. I had asked Prerana (a classmate and Vivek's dear friend) to add me to the group. And once I had saved his number, I left the group. This was the extent of my lovesickness. *Not lovesickness, you fool. Pathetic*!

Me: Vivek, do I have something on my face? Am I looking weird? Look at my face and stop staring at your phone.

Vivek dropped his phone. Oh I hadn't realised he would be that shocked. It was a perfectly normal request, no? Or maybe not. As he picked up the phone, he looked at me – his smirk intact and so was the raised eyebrow. And the dark cloud on his face had lifted completely. Damn he looked better when he was brooding and not this bloody smart alecky. Someone feed him three/four of those croissants please! After what felt like an eternity (even though it was less than a minute), my phone beeped. V: You always look weird and funny, Oinks. No, you don't have *goo* stuck on your nose or anywhere else. Why?

Phew. That was a relief. Or maybe not. Rajat was probably just spacing out then.

O: *Na*, nothing. Just got conscious. Whom are you chatting with since then?

V: *Aha*, curious to know? ;-)

Shit. Seriously. Did I have to let him know that? What an idiot. Me. Not him.

Thankfully, Hawkeye had finished *baantoing* all the *gyaan* he had gained in his 45+ years and then pronounced his judgement. Yes, we could all go sightseeing on Wednesday. Yay. Not that I was too eager to gallivant around Shillong with this particular set of people. But a day without checking email and doing EOFA work sounded good. On this triumphant note, we finally called it a day!

16

Utter chaos. That's what the next morning turned out to be. No, not due to my crazy family and friends. It was pouring in Shillong, raining cats, dogs and monkeys to be precise. We were at breakfast, where I had given in to complete temptation and was having my second chocolate croissant (yes, those huge ones – they were absolutely delectable. Yum yum). Rajat, sitting across me, was basically singing praises about Mumbai and his exciting life there. This was in response to my major *rona* about the *kuttas* and Ma and Baba. No, I hadn't told him about Ankita. I was too nervous about that whole situation. There had been absolutely no news on that front. Her elopement note had clearly said she would contact them soon. But when was that soon happening only God and Ankita knew. The previous night, after dinner, I had called Ma – and got completely yelled at.

"Tinku, you are calling now? Your cousin has been missing since the past one day."

"Ma, I was at work. I am busy. Official tour."

"Tinku, where is *Onkita*?"

"How am I supposed to know, Ma? Even that day at Flury's she hardly spent time with me. She left me stranded with that Vivek. Ankita has been very silent."

Wow. Ma listened finally to what I blurted out. "*Theek ache*. In case you hear anything, tell us. And do speak to Mamu-Mami."

Which is what I did and my heart broke into many miserable pieces. Mamu-Mami sounded so forlorn. I felt so guilty myself that I apologised. I would do anything to make them feel better. In case that Ankita girl ever came in front of me, I swear I would whack her. She deserved a solid beating for making Mamu-Mami go through this shit. And then I thought, with all this going on, somewhere at the back of my mind, what was the point in my simply worrying? Fuck-all I would anyway not be able to help from the wet, rain-soaked Shillong. Hence, I was focussing on those delicious, chocolatey croissants and also lapping up all that Rajat was saying to glorify Mumbai. The last few months, he had been trying to lure me to the 'City of Dreams'. Now, hearing about the *kutta* crisis at home, he intensified his efforts. I was, however, not interested. Life in Delhi was way too comfortable. Yes, despite the *kuttas* to take care of; and the EOFA job. I told him that but he wasn't convinced. Nonetheless, he continued with his efforts tirelessly.

At the table by the window, Aparna was seated, with a cup of hot *chai* in her hand, and looking dreamily outside. Vivek was also seated at the same table, drinking a cup of something hot, but was focussed entirely at his phone. By now, I was nearly dead – both of boredom and curiosity. Was it even possible? Exactly whom was Vivek messaging day in and day out? Who was she? It had to be she. After all he was supposedly engaged.

That was what I found out the previous night. You see, a lot had changed since then. All in my head, btw. Since Ankita and Sweety both were absconding and caught up in their own shenanigans, it meant that there was no one left to give me any sane advice. So, I teetered on to the dark side. I reached out to Prerana (on text) – the same girl from school, Vivek's friend who had kindly added me on to the school group. I wanted to know and confirm whether Vivek was still dating Shreya – my ex-bestie. Instead of asking her that, I went the roundabout, smart way and spent half an hour getting updates about the world and its aunties! And then, I messaged the most important question.

Me: Btw, do you remember Shreya Malkani?

P: Oh yes, you guys were best friends once upon a time, no? Then what happened? You kinda just lost touch?

Me: Ya, ya. I lost touch with all of you post 12th. Trying to reconnect finally ☻

P: Cool, btw she got married last month. Did you know?

Fuck. Was Vivek married? Had I missed seeing the ring on his finger?

Me: Ooooh that's so cool. Where is she? Whom did she get married to? Anyone we know? I don't even remember whether she was dating anyone back then.

LIAR LIAR PANTS ON FIRE!

P: *Na, re.* Don't think you know the guy. She met him in college and dated him first year onwards. Bharat Vaswani.

OH! First year. Wait, wasn't she dating Vivek back then? Served the bugger right. For jilting me and choosing Shreya. She must have cheated on him. What a mess.

Me: *Na*, don't know him. Do share her number with me. I am on a major reaching out spree.

P: Oindrilla, do you by any chance remember Vivek Rao?

Gawd! May the Lord Almighty grant me the fucking strength to bear whatever she is about to spill. I took a deep breath and played cool. Not that she was there to witness it.

Me: Yes, kind of. The nerdy, scrawny South Indian chap. Bespectacled. Me think whose father had some software business. He was dating Shreya, no?

I must have typed and erased 100 versions of this message, largely in a bid to appear cool. And if I may say this, this did sound bloody cool.

P: Dating Shreya? No, not at all. They were good friends. That is what she told me. Plus, I don't think he would disagree either.

Me: Oh cool. Good for him. What about him?

P: By the way, I was wondering whether you kept in touch with Vivek Rao after school.

Why on earth would I keep in touch with Vivek? I ran away to Delhi because of him. To avoid him.

Me: *Na*, not at all. Haven't been in contact with anyone really, except you.

There was a long pause. I thought the conversation was finally over. Till this message popped up 15 minutes later. And I died. Of complete shock.

P: Actually, I think can say this now. He used to have a major crush on you back in those days. And after school, he tried to locate you rather frantically. None of us had any clue where you were. Shreya told me this. He was forever in a spree to find out more about you from her. Last heard, he was about to get engaged or had just gotten engaged. Funny it was.

Me: WHAT?? I had no clue. But then, it was in another lifetime. *Chal* I gotta go. Catchya later!

So, you see, folks, post this shocking, life-altering information provided by Prerana, I couldn't sleep. Not a bit. I was agitated, nervous and on a short fuse by morning. Such a *tatti* life. Had this input reached me years back, what all could have happened!

Stop thinking about what could have happened. Well, for one, you idiot, you wouldn't have studied Korean! Maybe you would have gotten a decent, worthwhile education. Vivek is engaged. He keeps looking at the phone 24/7. Be professional, Oinks. You are here to work, finish the implementation and leave.

By the time I went down for breakfast, after 45 minutes in the gym, and a 30-minute walk near the hotel (despite the slight drizzle), throughout which the mental struggle continued, I was not only thus conflicted and agitated, but also exhausted. No news, good, bad, or ugly from home didn't help either. With nothing much to obsess about, no solid work (I had even cleared the bloody inbox), the only fucking thing in my head was Vivek.

The first person I met in the elevator.

"Hello, you are down early?" I squeaked, rather meekly.

He shot me a weird look.

Oindrilla, you idiot. Stop croaking, will you? Breathe in, breathe out. And DO NOT SPEAK if you have nothing intelligent to say. He is an engaged man. About to be married. Even if he had a crush on you. Back then. Which was many moons ago.

"It is 8:30 a.m. Not early," he replied. His phone beeped. Good god, his morning cooing had begun.

Luckily for me, we had reached the cafeteria where I spotted Rajat. Leaving Vivek to his phone and his long-distance fiancé, I walked up to greet Rajat enthusiastically (actually it was bit much, even according to me) in a bid to banish Vivek from my thoughts.

If only. Despite digging into two large croissants and 2 muffins and listening to Bombay's irresistible charms, I kept looking at that bloody Vivek who was STILL typing away to glory.

Abe how much do these engaged people chat?

"Oinks, you said something?"

FUCK. Was I too loud?

"Na, just muttering to myself," I covered up with a giggle. Which was too loud. Also hysterical.

Vivek finally looked up from the phone, looking rather confused, upon hearing my giggle.

It was then that Hawkeye got a call. Hawkeye, a slightly late entrant for breakfast, had then seated himself next to Aparna. And was trying to expound some major philosophy about the food in front of her. Even though Aparna had a smile on her face, she was clearly looking bored. She kept looking out of the window. God, how much will he try to impress her? And if only he would take a hint. Previously, well only a few weeks back, when I was the bitchier version of my current self and when Aparna was NBA, I had actually assumed that she was the one flirting with Hawkeye. Now seeing and observing her at close quarters, I have gathered that the poor lady was being nice. I make a mental note to confess to Tejas that I was wrong about NBA and probably even OBA! He was right.

The call had a miraculous effect on Hawkeye. He stopped eating and looked fucking serious. As if all the world's problems fell upon his shoulders. After the call, he solemnly looked around and composed himself. Good lord, this man loves the drama! Fuck it, can he just get on with it? What a slow motion announcement this turned out to be. He cleared his throat and said, "Ladies and gentleman, there has been a slight change in plans today. We can't meet the officials at the CDPO at 10 a.m. Our meetings have been pushed to tomorrow."

Finally, Vivek looked up from his phone, only to ask, "Why?"

"Oh, the rains have caused some landslides in the area. The entire roads are blocked; especially the ones that will lead to the *anganwadis*."

"Essentially then, we have the day off, today instead of tomorrow," interjected Aparna, coming straight to the point.

Hawkeye nodded, solemnly. He nodded some more, only to add, "I was wondering what sightseeing we would be able to do considering the rain and the landslides."

What the effing hell is this! All this drama for nothing. Well, I rolled my eyes and looked around to see if anyone else found it incredulous. Turns out Aparna did. I caught her eye and she had that small smile on her face. My phone beeped, a few seconds later.

A: Seriously. Much ado about nothing. You wanna go out for a walk after breakfast?

Me: You bet!

That solved a major dilemma. I had no fucking interest in basically moping around in my room – wondering mainly about who Vivek's fiancé was. My phone beeped again. This time it was Ma.

Ma: Did *Onkita* call you? There is no sign of her. Filing a police complaint.

Oh boy. It was then that the full fucking seriousness of the situation struck me. My cousin, baby cousin, sensible girl had eloped. Apparently. However, even after 24 hours since the supposed elopement, there was no news of her. What if she had been kidnapped by this lover boy Prabhas instead? For her supposed wealth and property? What if she hadn't been kidnapped at all? What if she had left home and then got hit by a truck? And was lying in a hospital, uncared for, unidentified? What if lover boy Prabhas was waiting for her still, in the rain?

A feeling of dread settled in my tummy as these weird probabilities crossed my head. Excusing myself from the table, I headed towards the gardens and called Ma from the porch. The conversation was short and intense. I did the listening. She did the talking. In a nutshell, no one had any clue where Ankita was. And hence the cops had been intimated. "Ma, do you know who Ankita has run away with? Maybe we can trace the guy, his family?" I haltingly asked Ma.

"Haan, she has run away with Bahubali."

"What?"

"That's his name I think."

"Ma, are you sure?"

Now who the fuck was Bahubali? What a new googly to deal with. I didn't know this fucking Prabhas character. On top of which, I had to look for a Bahubali, instead. And then it clicked, typically, like a tubelight that I was: Ma meant Prabhas only. For wasn't the actor who played the main role in Bahubali named Prabhas? Phew, my cousin wasn't dating one gentleman and eloping with the other. However, the question still remained – where was Ankita?

17

After that frantic call with Ma, I tried Ankita's number for a change. It rang and rang and rang. She didn't pick up. Why didn't Ma use her network and get the number tracked? Why hadn't they tried that? I immediately called Ma back to make this ingenious suggestion. "Brilliant. why didn't we think of this? Why didn't you tell us earlier?"

"Ma, the guy's name is Prabhas. Do you know his full name?"

"Oindrilla, of course I know his name is Prabhas. I told you that 5 minutes back. *Na*, no clue about his surname or *daak naam*!

My mother, as you can see, was as weird as I am. Suddenly I was plagued with a sense of guilt. Instead of obsessing over bloody Vivek, I should have given the matter of Ankita's elopement some serious thought. If her phone was ringing, it was possible that

a) she was not picking up known numbers or
b) she was in grave danger and her phone is lying somewhere else.

Before I gave my hyperactive imagination any further leeway, I decided to strike out option no 1. I needed to have someone else call Ankita. And since no one else knew Ankita or the predicament she had landed herself in, that someone else here in Shillong had to be only one person: Vivek. Bonus, I got to talk to him as well, provided I don't make an ass of myself.

I started walking towards the café – which is where I had last seen Vivek anyway. When I bumped into Rajat, who was apparently looking for me.

"Oindrilla, why don't we go for a walk? You aren't busy now, are you?"

Oh shit, had I not made similar plans with Aparna a while ago?

"Would love to, Rajat. But not now. I have some things to take care of immediately. Oh by the way Aparna and I also were making some similar plans. Why don't you join in? By the way, was Vivek still in the café?"

"Vivek? That PMU bloke? No, he went off to his room a while back – shortly after you left the café?"

"Oh ok, cool. Catch you in a bit."

Uh oh, this was a complication. I didn't know which room Vivek was in. I didn't know if I should find out and barge in. *What if...? OINDRILLA – STOP IT. Focus. You need his help. Entering his room does not mean landing up either in his arms or bed! REMEMBER – he is an engaged man. What if his fiancé was already in his room, arms and bed!*

After battling with such disconcerting thoughts for 15-20 minutes, with absolute butterflies in my stomach, I sent Vivek a message:

Me: Where are you?

And waited ... waited ... and waited for a reply which came only after a whole ten minutes later. What the fuck was he doing?

V: Room.

Huh? That is all? Was that even a reply? It was! To my idiotic question.

Me: Which one?

Brilliant. Oindrilla Roy, you deserve whatever award there is for asking the most idiotic of questions. Enough to drive this or any man far away from you. Facepalm! Gosh, where were Sweety and Ankita when I needed them.

Before I could delete the above mentioned inane question, he had seen it and was typing a reply.

V: My room. Oinks, what do you want?

Hmm, I mulled replying 'you' to the above question. But better sense prevailed.

Me: Need help. Is it ok if I come over?

V: Sure. 302

Phew. This meant that fiancé was not in said room or bed for now. Cos had she been, he wouldn't have responded promptly. Idiot. Vivek travelled alone or rather with that Ishita. You saw him at the bloody airport. Oops. Was Ishita his fiancé? They were rather chummy and all. Idiot. Focus.

Within no time, I found myself in front of his room – which wasn't a big thing considering it was two rooms away. On the same floor.

"Hi," I beamed, breezily, as Vivek opened the door. Looking absolutely yummy. He smiled and motioned me to enter.

"Yes, Oinks. What is the matter? How come you are reaching out to me? Your dear friend Rajat was unable to help?" Vivek was smirking again.

Dear friend? Rajat? Good friend, yes? But dear? Wait, do I sense a wee bit of jealousy in the question? Dare I even hope? Focus! Idiot! Focus.

I gaped, unable to spout out a reply. So much for being an adult, a professional, an educated young lady of the bloody 21st century.

"Rajat is a good friend. But anyway, you know about Ankita, no? That stupid girl isn't answering any one's calls. Her phone has been switched on again. I was wondering, if you could call her. Since she doesn't know your number, she might pick it up?" I said, all in a big hurry, sitting down on the chair nearby.

Vivek seated himself on the bed, which is where he would have been, probably watching Netflix – the laptop and phone both were there too. He listened carefully and nodded.

"Give me her number."

I rattled off the number and then added, "Were you watching Netflix?"

He looked up at me, surprised, and then went back to dialling the number. "One thing at a time, please."

The phone apparently rang for a while and then someone picked up!!

"Hello, may I speak to Ankita, please?"

"Ankita, hello, this is Vivek, Oindrilla's friend. Please don't hang up. We have been worried sick about you."

Oh great, she had picked up. She was also having a conversation with Vivek. I couldn't hear what she replied. But Vivek looked concerned and was listening intently.

"Hmmm, ok. I get that. Now exactly where are you? Ok. Give me a second. No, Oindrilla isn't here with me." He looked up and glared and placed a finger on his mouth. Motioning me to stay silent. Lest I yelled or behaved the way I usually did.

What followed was a long conversation, by the end of which we (*Vivek, that is*) had Ankita's exact coordinates. By the time, their conversation got over, I had started pacing the small room up and down out of sheer impatience and curiosity.

"Sit down, Oinks. I won't tell you if you keep walking up and down," he said curtly, when he finally cut the call.

"That's not fair, Vivek. It is terrible. She not only answered when you called but she also confided in you. I am her cousin, mind you."

"Yes, a hyper and a slightly crazy one at that."

"Ok fiiiine, now tell me where is she? Is she ok? What is going on?"

It turned out that lover boy Prabhas was not what he seemed. Meaning that while Prabhas's day job was that of a professor in some university in Cal (one of those new, arty-farty ones that have sprung up everywhere in the country, all international and all promising superior world-class education), he was in reality a big shot Naxal leader! He had wooed Ankita, knowing that she was an only child. He was in need of dire funds for carrying out activities on behalf of his breakaway Naxal faction group. Poor Ankita had fallen for his idealistic speeches, fiery passionate utterances (both otherwise and in bed) and had had been persuaded to elope (with her wealth in tow) by this rascal. Now on the day of the elopement, Ankita had a change of heart and she didn't take the jewellery with her. Prabhas was mighty disappointed, so thoroughly disappointed that he spent an hour convincing Ankita to rethink and asked her, gently and persuasively to head home and come back with the money. Thankfully, my cousin did not fall into the trap. This persistent convincing, she found it strange. An hour after this session, she accidentally stumbled upon another shocking truth. Prabhas was not even his real name. His name was Abdul

Hameed and on top of it he was a much married man and also *do bacchon ka baap*!!!

This shocking discovery brought the girl finally back to her senses. She managed to outsmart him and run away. The embarrassed girl was holed up since then in a *chhota-sa* hotel in Siliguri.

Her phone had been deliberately switched off. She didn't want to be found by the rascal Prabhas *urf* Abdul Hameed! She was fast running out of money. Now it was this reason why the phone was back on and she picked up Vivek's call. She needed help. By the time Vivek finished recounting his conversation, I was livid and ready to break the lover boy, no make that, rascal boy / Naxal boy Prabhas *urf* Abdul's head.

"Calm down. Now we need to act first, Oinks and get Ankita back home. You can fulfil your murderous fantasies later."

He had a point. I called Ma and Mamu, got them both on a video call and apprised them of the situation. At some point in time, Ma heard Vivek's voice in the background.

"Oindrilla, *tumi kothai*? Where are you? I heard a male voice. Who is there?"

"Ma, that's Vivek. My friend from school," I blurted, slightly breathless. And terribly embarrassed. Shit. What if Ma said something totally inappropriate and messed up my recently resurrected and budding relationship.

Relationship?? What relationship?? Everything is in your mind, you fool! The past, present, future.

While I was clearly flummoxed and aghast, Vivek was extremely unfazed. He made an appearance on the video call, right behind me and greeted Ma and Mamu warmly, with a Namaste!

"Hello, auntie, I am Vivek. We met that day on the flight, remember? Oindrilla and I were in school together; we are colleagues now. We are working here on the same project. Oindrilla asked me to call Ankita as she wasn't answering any of her calls."

Ma looked a bit concerned. About what I didn't know and did not want to ask. Lest she say something that would make me want to sink right through the ground like Sita! But thankfully, she nodded and mouthed a 'Thank you'. I was relieved.

Call over. Message passed. Ankita had been located. Phew. My turn then to thank Vivek.

"Thanks a ton, Vivek. Much appreciated," I smiled at him. It was truly heartfelt. He looked at me, without a smirk, but with some other kind of intense feeling in his eyes. I felt the butterflies again in my tummy and felt my toes curl up. He was quieter and more reflective than usual. And looked like he was about to say something. Not frivolous, rather something serious. When his phone started ringing.

"Oh that must be your fiancée! Is she here?" I said, breaking the extreme breath-taking eye lock.

"Huh?" My what?" Vivek had a confused look on his face. He looked at his phone and said, "It's your boss."

It was Hawkeye. Thank God it wasn't his nameless, faceless fiancée!

"Hello Vivek, where are you? In case you are free, would you like to join us for a round of sightseeing? *He he he*. Aparna and I will meet you in the lobby in the next 30 mins. It should have stopped raining by then ... *he he he*."

That aggravating nasal *He he he* was back! Can someone, anyone please tell him that it sounds bloody condescending and patronising and certainly NOT friendly.

"Thanks, Rahul. Would love to join. I will meet you in the lobby then. I saw Oindrilla head towards the gym. Why don't you drop her a message? She may not answer your call," Vivek glibly said, with a smile on his face. Knowing that I would dumbly retort, he put a finger on his lip, warning me to keep my mouth shut!

Shoot that was warning enough. I was about to retort. Vivek cut the call and then looked me up and down. Causing my heart to beat louder and faster than ever before. And just as I was getting all sorts of expectations up (*yes, I do have a gutter mind*), Vivek said, "Don't you think you should wear something sensible? For the tour? At least a pair of decent walking shoes?" *Phus* … what a deflating feeling those words brought upon my wildly beating heart. (Oindrilla Roy, you are pathetic.) Please do not infer that I was less than decently clad. It was just that I was walking around in a pair of bathroom slippers. My room was 2 rooms away remember? Suddenly the thought of exploring the beautiful locale with Vivek next to me (not literally for sure) made me elated and I hurried back to don a pair of walking shoes.

18

Half an hour later, I reached the lobby to find Aparna and Hawkeye engaged in a close discussion. Hmm, it couldn't really be termed a discussion. Hawkeye was pontificating upon something and Aparna was feigning interest. Upon spotting me, she cheerfully said, "Look, Oindrilla is there." Hawkeye turned towards me and continued his lecture. Poor lady. She needed to be rescued. I quickened my pace to get to them when I was waylaid by someone. It was Rajat. Smiling brightly he added, "It is so good to see you again."

"Again? We saw each other barely an hour ago," I blurted, slightly bugged.

"Yes, but still. It is always good to see you." he said, shyly. *What the bloody fuck? Was Rajat Bhat, my friend, my buddy, flirting with me? Was he interested in me?* However, before I could think or say anything, I heard my name being called out. Again. Loudly. It was Aparna. A clear plea for help. I excused myself and hurried towards Hawkeye – who, as expected, was going on and on like a broken record and Aparna, who had a bored-to-death expression on her face. Rajat followed me, quietly, without saying a word. *Weird!*

This Shillong trip was turning to be a dramatic one for sure – what with Ankita almost eloping with a Naxalite; Sweety and Divya eloping with each other; Prerana reminding me of my monumental blunder and Vivek's present engaged state; and now Rajat suddenly turning into a lover-boy. I needed a friend – a pure, unadulterated friend, who would listen to me and knock some sense into my head. Not a lovesick lamb who complicated matters. Fuck.

"Are you okay? You look rather lost," Aparna asked me. She had walked up to my side, while Hawkeye moved his attentions to Rajat! Phew!

I smiled simply. She looked at me rather closely and said, with a kind smile, "You look worried. In case you want to speak, I am here."

"Oh that's kind of you. Yes, I will. Thanks. Are we waiting for someone?"

I changed the topic. Moreover, I couldn't spot Vivek, who usually was punctual. *Usually? When? How do you know, you dolt? Because he would reach school on time (which was largely because of the school bus being on time) does not fucking mean that he was punctual. Stop it, Oinks. The man is engaged. The man is engaged. And there are more fish in the sea. Like Rajat. Oh God. But he is cute too. You thought so last year. Or was it because Vivek was NOT there last year? Damn you, Vivek!*

"Waiting mainly for the tour guide."

Oh. Where the fuck was Vivek then?

I pretended to look around and then casually added, "Vivek from PMU also doesn't seem to be around."

"Vivek? He was here but then he got a call. He has asked us to call him once the tour guide shows up. And there he is.

That must be the tour guide." Aparna looked towards the door of the hotel, where a young gentleman had just entered. He was looking around, rather unsure, of whom he was trying to recognise and locate.

"Should I call Vivek, then?

FUCK. Where did that come out from? What a faux pas!

The smart lady that Aparna was, she immediately caught on to it. Turning to me, slowly, she said, "Do you guys know each other – you and Vivek? From before I mean?"

And since I am an extremely bad liar, and there was no Vivek to smoothly side-step this question, I did what I do best. Nod and gape. Basically, I looked like a dying duck.

To my surprise, Aparna let it pass; more because the youngish gentleman – the supposed tour guide – was walking towards us. Noticing him, for the first time, Hawkeye stopped his monologue (this time with Rajat being the targeted victim) midway and took charge of the overall situation.

"*He he he*. Hello, hello! I am Rahul. I called you." He said, beaming his most beatific smile at the puzzled young man, who didn't respond. He simply stared back at Rahul.

"You are tour guide? You will take us out in cab." Rahul continued his attempts to get to the young man.

"Me? Tour? No. I cab driver. I look for Rahul. You Rahul?"

It was Rahul's turn to look puzzled. Isn't that what he had said too? He extended a hand and added, "We want to see all of Shillong. 5 people. Your cab big enough?"

"No, I not take you to Shillong. I come to give you this. CDPO office said to give." The man handed Rahul a huge file. Rahul looked at the file, fully deflated, and slightly bugged. Before he could even ask what that file was about, the man bade goodbye and left.

We continued to wait. Aparna had a tough time controlling her laughter, which she smartly camouflaged as a coughing bout. The gallant Rahul left to fetch her a glass of water, which is when we both burst out uncontrollably. "This was funny. Really, this Rahul can be quite a pompous guy – not a bad sort though," she said as she wiped her tears away.

"You bet. What were you being lectured about? I had assumed that was a sole privilege reserved for me alone – to be lectured by Rahul 24/7. I thought you were good friends."

"I speak to him, yes but I would not call him a friend. I speak to most people. Would have with you also, had you not stonewalled me like that." Aparna laughed and replied with a wink.

"I do not speak to most people," I quipped, slightly embarrassed. As Rahul came back with a bottle of water, arranged specially for a 'coughing' Aparna, another gentleman, looking equally lost, made an appearance. He walked up to us and said, "Tour people?"

Aha! Finally, our tour guide was there. Rahul once again assumed charge and spoke charmingly to the man who was called Mr R.B. Norbhum. After 10 minutes, the entire itinerary had been chalked out for the day. Mr Norbhum, who insisted we call him that, had suggested 3 or 4 key places that we must, should, and definitely visit. He spoke glowingly about the beauty of Shillong and the amazing sights 'The Scotland of the East' had to offer. The others listened with rapt attention, while I was jittery and nervous. Everyone, but me, had forgotten about Vivek. Where was he? After shushing my forever critical mind, on an impulse, I messaged him.

Me: Not coming for this tourist thingie? The guide is here.

A reply came almost instantaneously.

V: Coming. In a bit of a spot.

Me: What happened? Something serious?

V: Will tell you later. A crisis. Personal.

Ooooh oooh. Dare I hope? Did he fall in love with me? And then in filmy style, told his dear fiancée that he can't marry her? Oinks mera saccha pyaar hai! Eeks. That sounded so inane. It is the name – my name – Oinks. No wonder Hindi movie names are usually Pooja, Simran, Kiran, Nisha, etc., to make these corny, cheesy dialogues sound more believable!

My phone started ringing, rather loudly, putting an end to my idiotic flights of fantasy. It was Sweety. *Wow. Shit.* I pondered for a second whether to pick it up or not – the goddamn ring tone was too loud. I couldn't bump the call.

"Phone, Oindrilla. *He he he*. Don't behave like this with your boyfriend. *He he he*." Who else? Annoying Hawkeye, who thought he was being funny. Except that there was no humour in that nosey, intrusive remark of his. Which also turned out to be the only remark Vivek heard, as he walked up to join the party. Which I saw, as I excused myself to go and receive the call.

"Hmm, Sweety. Yes?"

"Divya and I will be there soon. Which hotel?"

"*Hein*? You plan to come and stay with me? In MY ROOM?"

"No, are you mad? Divya and I need some privacy, you dodo. Separate room. Same hotel."

"Look, Sweety, I am in a bit of shock. Ok. I kind of had accepted your relationship. Have you guys really eloped? But why? Doesn't make sense to me."

"I will explain when I get there. Now you tell me which hotel."

"Hotel Rosewood. I am in Room 304. O dear I missed you so much," I said as the call ended.

"*Arre*, Oindrilla, *apne* boyfriend *se baad mein baat karna*. Let us go." Fuck. I hadn't realised that all four of them (including Vivek) were just behind me when I was telling Sweety how much I had missed her!

19

After all those delays, partly caused by me as well, we set out on that sightseeing tour! We were to follow the same whole day itinerary that had been drawn up. By now, though I seriously was in no mood. Not only was the whole Sweety-Divya fiasco playing on my mind, I was also severely claustrophobic. The thought of packing ourselves tight in that Innova for the next fucking eight or however many hours was enough to spoil my not-so-good mood.

Good Lord, why was I even on this stupid sightseeing expedition, I wondered, as we got in and finalised seating arrangements in the Innova. Hawkeye seated himself next to Mr Norbhum; enthusiastically chatting him up – asking inane questions, replete with his unmistakable *he he he* – and definitely not discouraged by the silence from the other side! Aparna and I were in the middle; while Vivek and Rajat got stuck in the rear seat (the most uncomfortable of them all).

In a rare moment of being civil and nice, I actually offered to sit in the rear seat; after all I was the smallest (in size). However, Rajat had transformed into someone I hadn't witnessed before, a gallant, chivalrous chap, offering to sit instead! Why he even tried to help me get into the car. Seeing my irritated expression, Aparna commented, "Rajat, I am sure Oindrilla can get into the car herself. Isn't it so, Oindrilla?" Rajat turned beet red and quietly slumped into the back seat, where Vivek was already seated. Of course, duly stuck to his phone! It was almost as if that goddamn phone was an extension of his hand, without which he couldn't exist. I suddenly got bugged and had to fight the urge to yank his phone away. Better sense, which anyway was in short supply, prevailed.

I whispered to Aparna, "Did we really have to go with this entire jing-bang?"

"I am wondering the same. Should we try slinking away?" I grinned. She winked and initiated a conversation with Hawkeye. "Rahul, *aap humein kya-kya dikha rahe hain aaj*?"

Ooh she does it with so much finesse. No wonder I thought she liked him!

Hawkeye preened. Someone to speak to, no, actually make that lecture to. That too a pretty woman. Grabbing the bull by its horns, Hawkeye launched into a monologue, clearly inspired by the Lonely Planet series on Shillong or the Wikipedia Shillong page.

Our first stop was to be the Shillong Peak. "Elevated at 10 km South, Shillong Peak is the highest point that offers panoramic views of waterfalls, and lush green Bangladesh plains. A fair amount of trekking will be required to reach the peak. I hope you women are wearing comfortable shoes. *He he he*! Oh yes, no cameras please."

Worried that he would have continued, non-stop, in the same monotonous drone for eternity, Aparna quickly intervened again. She smiled her prettiest, gayest smile and said a gushing 'Thank you'. Excusing herself, and citing an urgent matter, she pulled out her phone and messaged me!

A: Let's branch out, citing some excuse, at Shillong Peak!

Me: Yes please. I cannot listen to Mr Wikipedia the whole day.

A: Neither can I.

Me: And here I thought you were friends! Good ones at that.

Aparna smiled when she read this message.

A: Ha ha ha. Have to work with them. I try being nice ☻

For whatever reason, post Aparna's deft handling of the situation, Hawkeye became quiet. Other than occasionally trying to chat up Mr Norbhum, who continued to give him the cold shoulder. Effective method, I must say. I made a mental note to try this and ignore Hawkeye when we are back at the office. Aparna continued to look at her phone – she was going through her Twitter feed – her face, expressing a thousand emotions, depending on what she read. In the seat behind us, where Rajat and Vivek were seated, there was an eerie silence. Curious to see exactly what the two men were up to, I looked back. Both of them had their earphones on and were looking outside the windows. What an odd bunch we were! Since I wasn't expected to engage with anyone, I let my imagination wander. Now that Ankita's sordid saga had been sorted kind of and I didn't want to speculate on Sweety's yet (there is time for that still), I wondered about Vivek's crisis. Whatever could that be? I found myself cooking up such fantastic scenarios – all with one end result. I was at an interesting point in a truly improbable (and exciting) scenario, where in I was battling some villains and saving Vivek, when I heard Aparna's voice. What was she doing here?

"Oindrilla, get up! We are here. At Shillong Peak."

Shit. I had dozed off again. Not only had I fallen asleep, I was also drooling – in front of all these people; including the object of one's fantasies (since forever)! How embarrassing was that. I wiped the drool off my face; the sleep off my eyes and profusely apologised. Aparna smiled, handing me a bottle of water.

"Sorry, sorry, it was too quiet. I fell asleep."

"Hey, it's okay. You weren't the only one dozing off. Rahul and Rajat took a short nap too. Only Vivek and I were up. Chill."

It turned out that we were waiting for the Air Force permit and needed to whip out our ID cards as proof. Mr Norbhum collected the ID cards from us and proceeded to get us the required permits. Once there, a short trek was necessary to get on to the peak. We stepped out of the car, stretched our legs and headed on the semi-circular path up.

Hawkeye walked right ahead, trying to be both boss and paternal figure of some kind. At office and at home, probably, he did the same. Or maybe not. Aparna and Rajat were right behind Hawkeye and bearing the brunt of his perpetual '*He he he*'.

"Stop making that face, Oinks. Too obvious." Oh Vivek, who was right behind me, had caught on to my shitty expression. An involuntary one when I heard the *he he he* for the billionth time!

"Hey, you feeling better now?" The dream had lingered on in my consciousness. My hero needed saving, didn't he?

Squinting his eyes, he said, "Yes." He looked down as we walked towards the rest of the group. He clearly wasn't comfortable.

Dilemma. Would it be okay to blurt out that I was extremely curious and had cooked up a million crisis-like scenarios (all of which by the way had me as saviour)? I mulled over this and decided that it may not sound right and may piss the man and shoo him away. Putting on my most concerned expression (*at least that's what I thought it was*), I softly said, "You were worried sometime back, no? Some crisis. Do you want to talk about it?"

Vivek kept quiet. (*Well when was he chattering away to glory?!!)* After what seemed like an eternity, in real time it was only a few minutes, he nodded and said, "Yes." After a long sigh and a deep breath, he added, "I am engaged. You know that, didn't you? Now make that I 'was' engaged." *Oh shit. Hearing him say that he was engaged made me wonder again. Why the fuck was I mooning over an engaged, taken man. (You idiot have been mooning over this man only for the last 100 years. Get a grip.)*

"Oh Ok. Congrats!"

"Congrats? Didn't you hear what I said, Oinks? I was engaged until this morning. I broke up with her. Nothing to congratulate me about," Vivek said, staring at me as if I had completely lost it.

Wait! What? I had lost him when I heard "I am engaged," I had somehow missed listening to his last sentence! Shit.

"You said you were engaged," I stuttered.

"Yes, up until this morning. And then we broke up."

"Oh. Why? Why were you engaged?" *OINDRILLA, you idiot, what a question to ask?* "Sorry, I meant why are you not engaged anymore?"

"Because I broke up. I just told you," He said, now grinning at this particularly absurd conversation.

What an intelligent conversation, indeed. I surely was going on like a nincompoop. Thankfully, I realised it and added, "Sorry this is a bit of surprise. I had heard that you may be engaged. Didn't know for sure. I didn't know you had broken up. Too much to digest in a minute. I am sorry, Vivek. Break-ups are awful. You need a hug."

To his and my surprise, I gave him a big, warm side-ways hug. He smiled and said, "It's ok. It's ok. I am fine. Besides your boss is looking at us with his mouth wide open."

To my horror, the moment I gave Vivek that impromptu hug, was also the moment Hawkeye looked behind to check on us laggards. His mouth was open. Very wide. I felt like stuffing a frog in his mouth! You see, I am not a friendly person at work or anywhere. Hell – I don't even like most people. Hugs, shaking hands or any form of informal contact was usually a big no-no. And here I was – hugging some colleague whom I supposedly met some days ago!

As nonchalantly as I could, without making a further fool of myself, I pulled myself away from a chuckling Vivek. At that moment I didn't know whom I would have liked to punch more – Vivek or Hawkeye. Who by the way was walking back towards us, looking too shocked.

"Oindrilla, Vivek, are you both dating?"

"What?! NO!" Both of us screamed in unison. A rebuttal, joint one at that, did bugger all to convince Hawkeye, who now continued to look at us – suspiciously – as if we were from outer space.

I was beginning to get annoyed, when Vivek cleared his throat and said, "Rahul, this morning, I got a personal phone call, which disturbed me no end. Oindrilla was checking upon that. When I told her what happened, she gave me a hug right away to cheer me up."

Wow. I never thought Vivek would launch straight into the crux of the matter and confide in Hawkeye of all the people. I continued scowling and stood there grumpily.

Hawkeye of course did not believe what Vivek said. He smirked some more, "Sure, I would like to believe you. But I also know her. She doesn't hug people just like that!"

Vivek smiled, as charmingly as ever and added, "Yes, she looks more like someone who would beat people up more! You see, my engagement broke off this morning. She got to know of it and was offering her commiserations."

Hawkeye's mouth fell. You see, he wasn't a bad sort. Just an old fuddy-duddy with outdated notions. He looked rather remorseful and immediately started apologising. "I am sorry. Vivek. You must be gutted." Saying which it was his turn to hug Vivek. And then it was Rajat's. Only Aparna stood at a distance and commiserated with him. She smartly figured that this unwarranted attention had made Vivek squeamish and uncomfortable. Finally, this unnecessary and uncalled-for scene got over and we started trekking towards the Peak. From where the entire city of Shillong was visible.

20

Now that we were headed towards the Peak, overlooking the city of Shillong, I suppose I should have been observing the beautiful scenery and sights around me. But that wasn't the case. Instead, I was struggling with the voices in my head. My curiosity as to what prompted Vivek's breakup had soon been replaced by an urgent message from Ma.

Crazy, weird people, the entire lot of them. No this wasn't the message that Ma had sent.

"Ankita back home. Girl has lost it. Go to Cal and help them."

Go to Cal? Was Ma ok? In her fossilised worldview, any job that wasn't with the government wasn't a job. It was a mere time pass. But still, I couldn't fathom what Ma wanted from me. What would I do going to Cal if *that* girl had lost it? Now I began to worry about Ankita. Now what had she gone and done?

I tried calming myself by focussing on the picturesque delights. Rajat and Aparna were laughing about something. Hawkeye had caught hold of Vivek and was giving him some useless *gyaan*. I am sure about heartbreak. Poor Vivek. He didn't have any choice but to put up with this shit. *All thanks to your impulsive gesture, Ms Roy! Who asked you to hug him?*

These people (however attractive two of them were in this lot) were certainly NOT the picturesque delights I wanted to focus on. Forcing myself not to think (and failing miserably), I looked around and was slowly dragging myself up ahead on the semi-circular path, when I heard someone call my name. It was Rajat. He was walking back towards me with a bashful smile. With two ice cream sticks in tow. Now this was weird. This guy, who had been a good friend a few months back, was behaving strangely. I am not generally a vain person – unlike some people I know, I do not think whoever looks at me was interested in me. However, Rajat's sudden interest in me, his constant staring, were getting a bit too much and making me uncomfortable. There he was now, walking towards me, with two ice-lollies in his hand. Huh? One of that for me? Turned out it was.

"Here you go. These looked yummy, Oinks. I thought you will like it," Rajat smiled as he handed one to me, his eyes, warm and adoring (*Oh oh oh. Banish those thoughts. Oindrilla Roy! Don't get unnecessary ideas.*).

I tried and after a few minutes succeeded as well. You see, Rajat and I had always gotten along. And there he was, passing some witty comments about the crowd, scenery, our colleagues, regaling me with laughter. After all the unnecessary drama, thanks to Ankita, which never seemed to end and the dread with which I was awaiting Sweety and Divya, this proved to be a respite. Methinks I laughed a bit too much, prompting the others to look at me. Including the brooding Vivek, who now, once again had a dark cloud on his face. Weird. Wait, why was he now frowning at me? Was he jealous by any chance?

How wonderful would that be. Before I could continue in this idiotic vein, my phone beeped rather loudly repeatedly – breaking both my train of thoughts and the silence around.

"Someone is trying to reach you desperately," Rajat laughed.

Uh oh. I was worried it was Ma again trying to bully me into whatever she wanted me to do with respect to Ankita and her weird situation. Darn. I whisked the phone out. It was not Ma.

It was Vivek. Holy holy Crap! Why was he messaging me?

I looked up, gaping still. That man was busy talking to Aparna.

I looked at the phone harder. Shit. It was not Vivek! You dodo. It was **Viveka** NOT Vivek. Wonder why she was messaging me desperately.

A much required digression – Viveka Mukherjee was a friend, once-upon-a-time. (Hmm, looks like the Vivek/Vivekas in my life are only exes – ex-friend/ex-crush/whatever.) Then we fought. About what I don't exactly remember. Ankita told me that in my drunken state after Grade twelfth, which I spent sozzled and sorry, more than anything else, I blurted out something (even she doesn't know what, because she was drunk too) and Viveka took offence. She stopped talking to me since that incident. We lost in touch and drifted apart. Ankita had messaged me about Viveka some months back. She had bumped into Viveka at some office. Right now, I had no clue as to why she was messaging me. Rather gingerly, I opened the message.

"Hi Oinks, remember me? This is Viveka. From school? Got your number from Prerana. Can you please call me when you are free? This is urgent."

Wow, wonder what she wanted from me. The rest of the messages were from – of course – my frenzied mother and that crazy friend. Shit, Sweety and Divya had landed up at the hotel. Already. Oh fuck. And I was at Shillong Peak.

I must have squawked rather loudly. Rajat was looking at me with a puzzled expression on his bright face.

"Are you okay, Oindrilla? You seem a bit perturbed."

"Uh oh umm, hmm, actually no. I need to talk to my mother. Oh and more importantly, I have to head back to the hotel."

"Oh but why?" Rajat looked a bit confused. Not surprising. I must have sounded utterly incoherent – I was clearly blabbering. You see, there were continuous messages from both those women. Ma and Sweety. And that was making me stressed, much stressed.

"My friends are here," I said, looking around.

"Here?" Rajat also started looking around.

"No, no, yes, I mean, they are in Shillong. At the hotel. Not here as in here. I have to go back."

"Ah ok. You have to go back," Rajat said, a bit too loudly.

"Who has to go back?" Aparna's voice butted in. Unnoticed by us, Aparna and Vivek had approached us.

By this time, I had gained some of my wits and senses back and managed to answer coherently.

"Hi Aparna, sorry, but I have to head back right away. Two of my friends are visiting me at the hotel."

Friends indeed! How could I tell her? My best friend Sweety and her lover (aargh) Divya had eloped and were parking themselves here, and had involved a reluctant me in their hare-brained, scandalous ordeal.

"Vivek, both you and Oindrilla can head back together."

Hein? Why Vivek? That didn't make sense. Shit. Did Aparna also know? Have I been staring too much with my lovesick eyes? Seeing me stare at her, probably a bit battily, Aparna continued, "Vivek has excused himself. He needs to get back too."

Vivek, who was standing next to me silently like a statue, and who, despite his goddamn nerdy good looks would have been completely ignored (because of his silence), nodded and added, clearing his throat. "That sounds good. Thanks, Aparna. Bye Rajat. You guys have a great time. Oindrilla, let's go."

Before I could count ten, I found myself in a cab, next to Vivek, and headed back to the hotel. Under any other circumstance, this would have been a dream opportunity come true – spending time ALONE with Vivek! However, my phone, no not phone, make that Ma had other ideas. No sooner had we sat in the car, the phone rang loudly. I answered gingerly only to be barraged by a volley of questions and complaints. It turned out that my cousin had disappeared. Again. When my uncle reached the address that Ankita had shared with Vivek, she was not there. They were about to register a complaint at the local police station, when they received a call from Ankita. Wherein she reiterated that she hadn't been kidnapped and that she was safe.

My frantic (and hence hysterical) mother wanted to know whether I had heard from Ankita. Which of course I hadn't. The conversation – mostly a monologue (*Ma's of course*) with occasional grunts and *naa* and *haans* from me – ended with me being fed a new set of instructions that I needed to carry out. By the time the call got over, I was positively thanking Hawkeye from the very recesses of my heart – I loved him, momentarily, for had it not been his idea to send me to Shillong, I would have been, at the very moment, trudging across roads and streets in rural Bengal, looking for my cousin gone astray.

I would have remained in that wool-gathering zone, imagining myself on the lookout for Ankita in a parallel existence, had Vivek not cleared his throat then.

"Hey, you okay? Things are fine?" he asked, with so much warmth in his voice and eyes that made my toes tickle. *Damn it.*

I explained the whole new development to Vivek, as clearly as I had understood from Ma. Vivek, very much in his element – you see, the man loves solving stuff – give him a problem and he dives right into the middle of action. *Oindrilla, how do you know? Well, he used to do that with exams and assignments. Hence. Idiot.*

Whatever it was, it looked like he had found something to distract himself from. He promptly called Ankita. Her phone was busy. "Well, she seems to be speaking to someone. Look, Oinks, if she is being communicative, then it will be fine."

He made complete sense. "Yes, you are right. She probably will call back. How are you now?"

"I am fine. Better. Wanted to get back because I need to make a few calls – all related to the damn fiasco. By the way, who are these friends who are over here? I overheard you mention that to your boyfriend a short while back."

My jaw dropped. Boyfriend? Who? Oh fuck. Vivek meant Rajat. No, No, No.

"Rajat isn't my boyfriend," I squeaked, as it was then that I remembered Sweety and Divya. About whom I had completely forgotten for all of 10 minutes.

With the annoying smirk and raised eyebrow back in place on his face, Vivek causally remarked, "Oinks, it is okay. You guys looked way too cosy together. No need to get flustered or embarrassed. You can tell me, you know."

Shit. That was not supposed to be his reaction. He should have turned green with jealousy. Oh but wait, was that the dark cloud look? *Oindrilla, stop it and set the matter right.*

"Vivek, you really have the wrong idea. Rajat is a friend, a good friend..."

"...who is in love with you."

"What?!" It was my turn to stare at him wordlessly. I recovered my composure, or so I thought, and hastily blurted out, "Look, look Vivek, you have got it all wrong. Rajat and I are not dating. He may or may not be in love with me. I don't know. And I am flustered because of Sweety and Divya."

"The friends?"

"Yes, yes, they are already here," I exclaimed, rather a bit loudly.

Vivek looked at me surprised, unable to comprehend, why was I looking like a dying duck. Looking at his puzzled expression, and because I needed to spill the beans and share this new mess that I had landed into, I decided to tell all.

"Sweety and Divya have run away from home. Together. To get married. And since they didn't know where to go, they are here. Sweety is my BFF, you see. She thought I would be able to help."

I waited to see how Vivek would react. But to my surprise, he was perfectly okay. Fuck. I am a homophobe. The man didn't even bat an eyelid.

"Umm, and they are here now. How do they want you to help them? Are you going to be a witness for their wedding?"

"Wedding? What wedding?!" I looked at him blankly.

"Oinks, what have they run away for then? If not to get married?"

"Are you not shocked?"

"About what? Two people eloping?"

"Hmm, two people of the same gender eloping. Are you not the least bit shocked?" I asked, querulously and suddenly nervous as well. God, I really am a closet homophobe and now he knows that too.

"Hmm, people's preferences, Oinks. I am not shocked. But I get it you might be. These are your close friends, I suppose."

"Yes, yes Sweety is. She has been a big support – especially when I was..." *IDIOT, what were you about to blurt out?*

"Hmm..." Vivek looked at me, a focussed look in his eyes. (*OK that was my interpretation*).

"Umm going through a bad phase some years ago."

"After school?"

"Umm yes." I looked away, suddenly feeling conscious and perturbed. This was getting bloody uncomfortable.

Changing the topic, as smoothly as I could, I muttered, "So Sweety announcing her elopement has made me uncomfortable. I do not know whether it is because she is dating a girl or that it is Divya that she is in love with that is bothering me. You see, Vivek, Divya is a complete bitch."

Vivek started chuckling. "Oinks, you have never really been a people person. What has this dame done to you? She sounds like someone I definitely would like to meet!"

I rolled my eyes. "Whatever. Divya is a complete bitch. Period. I do not like her." I would have continued and gone on to rant a LOT more about Divya to Vivek; however, at that very moment we arrived at the Rosewood Hotel.

21

And lo, who did we spot near the entrance? Sweety and Divya, giggling away to glory.

"Oh that's them," I said, pointing towards the two giggling girls, who were any way garnering quite a bit of attention.

Vivek looked at them, with interest, and chuckled. "Aha, the interesting, eloping couple. I thought they needed help. They look way too carefree. Are you sure they aren't pulling a fast one on you? I mean, knowing how easily shocked you are, easy to scare you into believing that they needed help. But in reality, they are out holidaying in picturesque Shillong."

"NO! Sweety would never do that!" I exclaimed. And then realised that Vivek was laughing a bit too much. "Come on, stop pulling my leg. If you can help me out, then do so. Else, please."

"Is the ever-so-independent Oinks asking me for help?" He continued, laughing some more. I didn't know whether to laugh or take offence. On one hand, I was chuffed. Vivek was talking to me, in a friendly way, and it felt good. But then on the other hand, what was I to do about the two women? The cab came to a halt in front of the hotel, just as I smiled back, rather sunnily, at Vivek. As we stepped out and settled the payment for the ride, Vivek put an arm around my shoulder and said rather sweetly (*oh my dear heart*!), "Don't worry. You aren't responsible for what these girls have been up to and will be up to."

"Huh, what do you mean? What have they been up to?" My dirty mind was racing in all sorts of directions.

"God almighty. The prudish Oinks has a dirty mind. Who would have thought of that?" Vivek was guffawing by now and that too loudly. "To clarify, Oinks, I was advising you to stop fretting about Ankita's antics and Sweety's shenanigans. Now I am off. Need to sort out stuff with my ex." Vivek said gently patted me on my cheek just before walking away. I froze. What the bloody hell was that. An affectionate gesture.

To my utter rotten luck, Sweety and Divya had also witnessed this gentle moment. Well, not only Sweety and Divya, but so had some bell boys and a number of guests. Sweety had her mouth wide open, while Divya had a smirk on her face. Oh gosh. This was embarrassing.

"Oinks, what was that?" Sweety demanded.

"Actually, more importantly WHO WAS THAT?" Divya butted in. *Could she please stay away? Some nerve really, this woman has. Oinks, not the time to be bitchy.*

"Umm, hi guys. Good to see you here. Let's go inside." I hugged the two women one after the other. Divya, only because I had to. I was in no mood to have my non-existent romance dissected there – standing in front of the Rosewood Hotel. To make my point doubly clear, I marched straight inside the hotel and walked towards the elevator lobby. Sweety and Divya hurriedly followed me, whispering something to each other and giggling. They followed me not only into the elevator but also into my room. The moment we entered the room, the volley of questions started.

"Who was he? Why was he hugging you? Are you dating him?" – All these were Sweety's questions. Divya seated herself on the chair in the corner and was observing me. Fuck. This was pathetic.

"Hey, hey, stop. Why am I the one being interrogated when you guys are the ones who have run away from home!"

The girls started laughing. "Oinks, did you really think that?"

FUCK! Vivek was right then!

"Wait, you haven't eloped?"

Sweety and Divya looked at each other and smiled. AGAIN. That's the only thing they seemed to be doing. These two.

"Listen, Oinks, this is bloody complicated. You know, Divya and I are crazy about one another. Now of course, while we may have technically eloped; our folks don't know that we have eloped."

"Huh? You are here. Surely they know."

"Oh yes, they do. We told them we are here to visit you. Because you are in some kind of trouble. And that you have reached out to us and asked us for our help!" Sweety said, looking mighty pleased with herself. "Without paying any attention to the expression on my face, she continued, "You know, I told Ma, that it was the same old Vivek story and that you are depressed. Sorry, ya. You understand, *na*?"

UNDERSTAND! My bloody foot! No I didn't.

"How the fuck could you do this to me, Sweety? Not cool at all." I was seriously pissed.

Sensing my anger, Sweety kept quiet while Divya sweetly interjected. "Our apologies. We should have informed you that we have told the folks that it was a holiday to cheer you up."

I could not believe what was going on. "And exactly when is this holiday of yours going to get over? When are you planning to drop the bombshell to your folks? About your relationship? Or will you be telling them that Oindrilla has coerced the two of you into a relationship?"

Looking a bit shamefaced, naturally, at my acerbic retort, Sweety gently said, "We were wrong about not warning you beforehand."

"Yes, Sweety, you should have told me that I was being made the scapegoat. The one who would be fielding all the questions from uncle and aunty."

"Sorry, darling." Sweety came and gave me a warm hug, which melted my anger away. Shit. I couldn't stay angry forever, could I?

"Ok, now what do you want me to do? You guys are on a holiday and then what?"

Divya started pacing up and down the room while Sweety looked terribly uncomfortable at this question. I really had no clue what was going on. After some painfully awkward, quiet moments, Divya spoke. "Oinks, the thing is my folks have found this guy they want me to marry. This trip is to buy some time in the hope that the guy will lose interest and break off the engagement. Maybe they will stop pressurising me to get married for sometime."

"What? You are engaged?"

"Yes!" Divya said mournfully.

What were these two crazy women up to? What was going on?

"Wait, when I left Delhi, you weren't engaged!"

"Yes, I got engaged two days back. Which is why we had to leave Delhi citing that you are heartbroken and needed help."

It did not make any sense to me. These girls were in a royal, complicated mess. Just then the phone rang. No not mine for a change. It was Divya's. "Oh good heavens, it's Abhishek. My fiancé."

Sweety screwed her nose up as Divya excused herself and took the call.

"Sweety, you okay with this situation?" I asked gingerly. To be honest, I was astonished at my friend's rather mellowed reaction. She didn't seem particularly pissed. I would have been if my lover had gotten engaged to someone else. Then again, she had run away with her lover girl and was here. What a complicated, confusing situation!

"Hmm, we did what we could, no? *Arre ab kya karein*? There was so much family pressure on Divya. Her dadi would have died pronto had she announced that she wanted to marry me. I get that. Hence."

Divya's call was over. She plonked herself on the bed where Sweety and I were sprawled out. She looked at Sweety (*with so much louw that I wanted to puke*) and said, "Don't think this Abhishek will be a hassle. He doesn't seem to be interested in getting married either. Worst case, I will get hitched and carry on with you on the side."

Sweety was now holding her hand and nodding. I nearly fell off the bed. "Whoa, fuck fuck." Both the women had completely lost it. "Hold on, no, you both certainly CANNOT do that."

They looked at me as if I were from outer space. "That is unethical. Downright immoral. Sweety, Divya, have you taken leave of your respective senses? Or did you never have any?" I know I was being harsh, however, how the fuck was I going to digest what they had mentioned.

Sweety, my best friend, my soul sister, had lost her head. She was going to be like a stepney, the third wheel in a marriage, and she seemed particularly blasé and nonchalant about this preposterous suggestion. Since I wasn't doing anything other than frothing at my mouth and giving myself an unnecessary heart attack, I walked out of the room. Only to bump into Vivek near the elevator.

"Hey, you ok? What happened?" Taking in my more-than-usual grouchy expression, Vivek asked. He also looked around, probably hoping to spot my eloping friends.

"Nothing," I snapped at the poor man and entered the elevator.

"Hmm, nothing happened. Then why are you snapping at me? I didn't do anything," he said, amicably, following me in.

He was right. The poor guy hadn't done anything this time. Why was I being my usually irritable self and taking it out on him?

"Sorry, Vivek. I shouldn't have snapped. It is all that Sweety and Divya's doing." Sick of the entire drama surrounding my cousin and friends, I blurted out, rather impulsively, "Are you busy now? Should we go for a stroll? I need to get away and not see their faces."

"Sure. I was heading out anyway for a stroll. What happened? What is it that is bothering you so much?

Poor Vivek. Without waiting for any further ado, I launched into a diatribe. Against Sweety and Divya. Against their complete thoughtlessness and the callousness of their hare-brained plan. He listened patiently without, thankfully, adding his two bits till I ran out of steam.

"Thanks, for listening. I needed to get that off my chest." I smiled, as we walked back towards the hotel. He smiled, that crinkly-eyed, heart-stopping smile, and patted my head. I probably stopped breathing for a second, and my heart went into a complete tizzy. As I looked up at him, I felt myself drowning into his warm, deep eyes. Was it my imagination, or was Vivek also looking at me with extra fondness? And what was that? Desire? *Yikes. Oinks, control.*

22

As Vivek and I stood near the gate of the hotel, staring into each other's eyes (ok, that is an exaggeration. It was only for a moment or so), I heard someone call my name. Damn it. It was Sweety. Who was closely followed by Divya. "Uh oh, these two girls again. Wonder what they will now get up to."

"See you later, Oinks. Maybe for dinner or something?" Vivek said, as he started walking away towards the hotel.

I didn't want him to leave; going by the way he turned back to smile at me, think even he didn't want to. But well. I smiled back at Vivek and then proceeded to face my crazy friend and her crazier partner.

"Where were you, Oinks? You walked away in a huff and we were worried," squealed Divya as they approached me.

"Who was he? Oinks, are you dating him?? You hardly got here two days back." That was Sweety.

"Shush shush, nothing like that. I am bugged, terribly bugged with both you women. I didn't want to see your faces for a while." I replied to them and started to walk back towards the hotel. *(PS: I hate conflict and this whole situation was making me terribly uncomfortable. I did not wish to be associated with their hare-brained, unethical scheme.)*

"We need to talk, Oinks. I know you are pissed with us. But can we speak like grown-ups?" Aargh who else would that be? But that supercilious Divya. She was right though in this case. My running away without speaking my mind definitely wasn't helping the situation.

"Hmm, we should. Let us head back to the room, then. By the way, which room are you booked in?"

Sweety and Divya looked at each other, now even more sheepishly. "Umm, we were wondering if we could stay with you. Just like back in the IIM days. Our luggage is in the cloak room!"

WTF! My eyes popped out of their sockets. I couldn't believe my ears. I certainly didn't want to spend the night with these two cooing love birds. Reading my ever-transparent face, Sweety added, "Look, if you aren't comfortable, it is okay."

Much as I hated the idea of having these two lovebirds in my room, I did not want to rebuff my best friend either. I merely nodded, "It is okay. Let us go. Come on."

Half an hour later, seated on the bed in my, now, our room, we tried to have an adult conversation – a conversation in which I did not roll my eyes, mouth abuses and cuss words, and tried to understand their point of view. A conversation which ended in a stalemate – kind of at any rate.

"Look, guys, you wanna get hitched. Be my guest. I will happily be your witness. But this subterfuge is certainly not done. Divya, YOU CANNOT marry that poor chap and ruin his life. Sweety, you wanna be the other woman in their relationship, seriously?"

Divya looked down and nodded. "I get it but I am shit scared. You know my folks, do ya? They will freak. NO one in the wide *Punju* Sehgal *khaandaan* of ours has ever come out. I do not know if I have the guts."

"Well, that's for you to gather and figure out. I am sorry, I cannot be party to any kind of duplicity." I concluded, with a flourish, mentally thanking Vivek. You see, it was him who had put some sense into my head. Left to myself, I would have either cussed or sulked, neither of which classified as adult behaviour. In fact, I wanted to go and thank him for that.

My long monologue, rational and composed, had its desired impact. Sweety and Divya were quiet and thoughtful. "Hmm, ok, we will think about and discuss, and see what we can and should do," said Divya, as Sweety sat with a strange look on her face.

"Now, you tell us, Oinks. Who was that guy? First he strokes your cheek, then you stand looking at him as if he were the only one on this planet. Spill. You seem to be besotted with this man! How on earth did that happen? You know, Divya, if I had realised it were that easy for Oinks to stop mooning over that school chap Vivek, I would have introduced many more men like this man downstairs earlier." Sweety looked at me pointedly, with a determined expression, demanding to know.

I hemmed and hawed and quite unsuccessfully attempted to evade the questions but then at the end had to blurt out, "It is Vivek!"

"What? THE Vivek?" Both their mouths were wide open. "Oindrilla Roy, spill all the details. RIGHT Now."

And over the next hour, all their shenanigans were forgotten in room no 304, as I recounted Vivek's re-entry in my life the past week. "Well, he isn't bad looking, I suppose, you can carry on with him." WTF, even the supercilious Divya approved of our so-called match and gave me her blessings. "Divya, Sweety, nothing is going on. We are colleagues, fairly sympathetic to each other, that is all."

My phone buzzed right when I was making this proclamation. Aparna, Rajat and Hawkeye were back and wanted to know whether I would be joining them and Vivek for dinner. We decided to go down too and join them, not before I had coached Sweety and Divya to behave themselves. No PDA, no ragging me about Vivek, only plain, prim and propah behaviour.

Dinner turned out to be exceptionally interesting. Sweety and Divya behaved themselves and how.

"Sweety, this is such a pleasant surprise! *He he he*. Who is this charming lady with you? *Arre* Oindrilla, *bataya nahin ki* Sweety was the one who had dropped by."

Sweety had worked at EOFA, remember? Hawkeye and she used to be in the same team and knew each other well. However, Aparna and Rajat had not come across Sweety. Introductions were made and we were soon seated at the table. Soon, the supercilious Divya, who was an expert at turning on her charm when she wished to, had Hawkeye eating out of her hands. *He he he*, he went throughout the dinner, focussing entirely on Divya, much to my amusement.

"How long are your friends here for?" Aparna asked me, as we were getting some food from the buffet counter.

"A few days, I think. They are here for a holiday. My presence is just a *bahana* to tell their folks back home."

"Ha ha, that is cool. Good you got to spend some time today, with them. Tomorrow onwards, work will get started on the project. Talking of work, exactly why is Vivek sticking to your other friend?"

I nearly dropped my plate at this question. Vivek and Sweety were huddled at a corner of the table and laughing about something. As I stared at them, Aparna continued, "Poor guy, he has been through hell today. Good to see him smiling. Though he shouldn't fall for your friend on rebound."

I merely nodded. Even though we were walking to the table, I had already stuffed my mouth an enormous slice of pizza and couldn't speak. The impatient person that I was. Besides what else could I say? That it wasn't Vivek who was sticking to Sweety but the other way around.

Though I must confess, I was curious. What were they laughing about?

"Is anyone sitting here?" Rajat asked, eager and friendly.

"No no, please sit."

"How was your day, Oindrilla? Did you have a great time with your friends? Good that we will get back to work. I missed you."

Huh? I stared at him shocked. What had come over him? From friend to suitor, Rajat was making a pretty fast transition. I wasn't sure whether I liked it though. At the cost of reiteration, I am not a vain girl. Never have I fancied people falling for me. Now that Rajat was making his intentions super clear, I was getting *maha* uncomfortable. Citing some excuse, mainly of stuffing my plate and eventually my mouth with more food, I scooted from the place. Not before, Rajat smiled and said, "You don't need to run because I embarrassed you with my frank admission about how I felt. Don't worry, bring some grub back. Won't raise the topic again. We can discuss, instead how your friend is fawning all over that poor Vivek."

Darn. Why the fuck was I so bloody transparent? I needed to quickly tell Rajat that I love him, completely, absolutely but ONLY as a friend. Nothing more nothing less. Before he got absolutely unbearable in this new avatar of lover boy.

23

I was absent-mindedly serving myself a second helping of risotto, when Vivek walked up to the counter.

"Hey, Oinks, there you are. Can you please ask your best friend to stop interrogating me?"

SHIT. Did she have to be THAT obvious? I knew that Sweety would try figuring out whether she liked him enough or not? Which would have involved many questions. A drill that she had perfected back in the days when I was remotely dating. My love / sex life had been rather non-existent the past year or more ever since I broke up with my previous boyfriend. And then there was no one at EOFA.

"Huh, whatever do you mean? Sweety is a friendly soul, eager to meet new people and all. She must be curious."

"What have you told her about me, I wonder? She is a bit too curious," Vivek chuckled. Changing the topic, he quickly added, "Is your little problem solved?"

"Not really. They have at least decided to think about it more before taking any knee-jerk action."

"That's good I suppose for the time being. Where are they putting up?"

"In my room." I said, not sure whether I looked unhappy or happy when I said that. Whatever my expression was, it must have been funny, because Vivek looked at me rather intensely and then grinned. "What is it, Vivek? Why are you smiling?" I asked, rather bluntly. I didn't get it why he was grinning.

He chuckled. "Everyone is expecting me to sulk and brood. Why? Can't I smile?"

"Your engagement broke up this morning, didn't it? Seriously, how are you feeling about that? I mean, I don't know." The smile vanished from his face. *OINDRILLA, you insensitive idiot!* "Hey, sorry, I didn't mean to hurt you. Sorry, forget I asked. You know me, I speak first, think later."

After a moment of stony, uncomfortable silence, Vivek said, "That you do – speak first, think later. I am okay. Or getting there. Don't want to talk about it now, Oinks. Will tell you sometime about the entire fiasco. Think we should go now. Your lover boy is shooting daggers and knives at me."

"He certainly is not my lover boy! Rajat is a friend."

"If you say so." Vivek walked away, laughing, and before I could follow him, Sweety waylaid me.

"Oinks, why are you spending so much time with this fellow?"

"Huh? Who?"

"Who? This Vivek?! I don't think I like him. I mean he is okay. He caused you so much heartache back then. I can't forget that. Instead of getting back at him or ignoring him and giving him the cold shoulder, you are laughing and getting cosy with him. This isn't done." Sweety hissed and glared at me.

"Gosh, Sweety, you are overreacting. We are merely cordial to one another. Also, please remember we are mature adults now. No point harping on the past." *Wow. I must admit*

I was impressed with myself. I sounded so poised and controlled. Must be something in the Shillong air. Or food. They must be mixing something in it.

"You are turning into even more of an idiot. A wool-gathering dimwit. I am not overreacting. I saw how heartbroken you were. As your friend, I cannot see you go through a dark phase again. On account of the same bloody guy. He may be ok but he caused you grief. Never. You don't have my blessings. If you want a distraction, look over there. Such a good looking, pleasant gentleman. That Rajat. He is the one for you." My nosey friend declared, right when we had reached the table. Had her interference been limited to only a suggestion it would have been ok. However, when was Sweety ever so subtle?!

After interrogating Vivek for more than half an hour, she seemed to have fixed her attentions to Rajat – who became the object of her intense scrutiny for the next hour. Rajat was surprised but was at his charming best. Smiling politely at Sweety and looking at me, sideways, with love-filled eyes. *Aargh.* Those uncomfortable (for me) affectionate glances that were being sent my way were most disconcerting. *Ugh.* This stupid Sweety was proving to be of no help either. They both had to be kept in their place – Sweety had to be packed off to Delhi, single or married; and Rajat had to be told to behave! The rest of the dinner kind of passed in a tizzy. I was, anyway, strategising my next move. You see, this whole bloody conversation with Rajat (telling him to behave and basically snubbing him) was bound to be terrible; I needed to dig into the reserves of my calmness and inner strength to face him. *Harumph! Inner strength indeed. Drama Queen – that was me. I know. I know. Can you, my conscience, my inner fucking mind give me a bloody break from your fucking commentary? Well done,*

Oinks. You are descending into your true potty mouthed self again. All is well.

Seeing how Sweety was continuing to hog all of Rajat's attention and going by the deep convo, anyone would have thought that she was interrogating him for herself! It surely looked way too cosy. Divya noticed it too for she kept throwing glances alternatively at the duo and me: jealous ones at them and questioning ones at me. As if I would know what that crazy Sweety was up to. If that was not bad enough, even Vivek did not spare me questioning glances. When I ignored and did not look back at him, he had the bloody temerity to message me.

V: Why Oinks, are you sure your Sweety friend is not interested in men? ;-)

V: Oinks, are you not jealous? Lover boy seems to have forgotten you completely! :)

I did what any mature adult would have done in my place. Glared at the man across the table and ignored the messages.

We were about to head back to the room. Sweety was still with Rajat. Divya was bored – poor girl, for all her bitchiness, spending an entire dinner with Hawkeye can be traumatising – I so do not blame her! Aparna and Vivek were discussing something animatedly. Dinner over, when we were about to leave, I impulsively came to the conclusion that it was better for me to walk up to Rajat and ask him to stay back for a serious conversation. But Sweety was yet to finish her marathon interrogation or conversation or whatever that was, I started walking with Aparna and Vivek. But just then my phone beeped again. It was a message from Viveka!

Oh bloody hell. I was supposed to have called her; or at least messaged. Quickly excusing myself, I walked out to the main lobby. It was quieter there to apologise first on message and then on a call.

Me: Sorry sorry, Viveka. I do remember you. Have had a busy day. Do let me know when we can speak. Maybe tomorrow around 10 a.m.? Good night.

Barely had I sent the message, it rang! It was Viveka.

"Hey, what's the matter? All okay? How have you been?"

"Hey, I am ok. It has indeed been a long time. Sorry, but I had to get in touch with you. You see, your cousin Ankita is now at my place. With me."

"WHAT?"

"Yes, it's a long story. To cut it short, I know Ankita and yesterday she called me out of the blue and asked me to help her. I think your folks and all must be worried. I have advised her not to answer her phone. You see, that guy may have gotten her phone tapped. Could you kindly pass on my address to her parents?"

"Oh yes, thank you. You are such a Godsend! Thank you thank you. You please WA your address. I will send it to Mamu."

Address and relevant details procured, promises made to meet, and gratitude expressed profusely, the call soon got done. Promptly after that I contacted Mamu-Mami, and Ma and updated them. They planned to reach Viveka's place and bring back Ankita almost immediately. Thank the Lord. At least one fucking mess had gotten resolved. I felt part of the load slide off my shoulders. Gawd. What a day it had been. I so needed a drink.

The universc was kind to me. I bumped into Vivek a minute later near the lift lobby and found myself back in the restaurant bar the next few minutes. Along with him. How I landed up in the bar with Vivek is a story in itself. He was looking a bit morose when I found him near the lift lobby. The mature, poised, adult me, instead of making a snarky comment, asked him with a lot of concern.

"What's the matter, Vivek? You look a little grumpy." *How bloody mature! Of course, he would look grumpy. It had not even been a day since his engagement ended. What did you expect, Oinks? He would be standing there, with stars in his eyes because you are there!*

"Hmm, nothing really. Do you care for a drink? Let's get one if you are up to it."

I couldn't believe what I heard. The universe was indeed kind to me.

"Yeah, sure, let's go."

And there we were at the bar. Not much was spoken. Vivek was quiet, reflective and definitely morose. I was exhausted and did not trust myself to speak anything sane or intelligent. Hence, I decided to shut up. After a longish silence, he finally snapped out of his reverie. "Sorry, I am not really the bestest of company at the moment. It has been a rather longish day."

Tell me about it! "Yep, it has. Too much action. Also tiresome ya. For you, much more, no? At least in my case, my engagement did not break." *FUCK FUCK FUCK. Did you have to blurt that out, Oindrilla Roy?*

As an expert in covering up post awkward foot-in-mouth situations, I quickly looked sheepish and squeamish and was about to make all the adequate conciliatory noises (perfected through years and years of practise), when Vivek spoke.

"Hmm, yes, it has been a tough day. Tougher than I thought it would be." He looked so lost and mournful that I didn't know what to do. I simply placed my hand on his – something that works with my lovely *kuttas*, Choco and Chipki. Oh god, I was missing them as well.

Vivek looked pleasantly surprised but he didn't either pull his hand away or push mine. That was good. I was silently pleased too. It was a nice feeling, trying and perhaps succeeding in comforting him. Somewhat maybe. After a long pause and silence, which was not awkward at all, Vivek spoke, "Thanks, Oinks. I know you are trying to help. I don't need much comforting, honestly. I am not gutted. I didn't think that my engagement to Aarti (hmm, that was her name) would even last as long as it did. My folks were keen to get me hitched to her. I went along. I am feeling rather bad for my mum. She has taken it real bad."

I was stunned. My standard response in any such awkward situation was to basically squirm and gape. Both of which I successfully did. What was I supposed to do or say? So much for my trying to play assume role of close confidante. The man didn't seemingly want one. Besides whatever did he mean, when he said he went along. Who goes along and marries anyone? In this day and age? Must be some weird custom in the Kannadiga community. I would never marry anyone my parents sent my way. Considering Ma and Baba were more bothered about *kuttas, kaam* and now Ankita, I was not in their radar and surely wouldn't be for a while.

"Sorry to hear that. If I may ask, why would you marry just about anyone?" Oh God, before I realised, I had blurted the question out.

To my great relief Vivek didn't find that question strange or too personal. He didn't react for a bit. Phew. Then he looked up from his glass and straight into my eyes. Intensely at that. Fuck. "Hmm, I do not know. Folks were keen ... I was not seeing anyone either. Come to think of it, I am relieved now, Oinks. I have had a lucky escape."

The intense look had done it for me. Butterflies were flitting about in my stomach like there was no tomorrow. And before I could do anything stupid, I thought it better to scoot. When all I wanted to do was throw myself in his arms. "Hmm, good that you are fine and aren't taking it that badly. Anytime you need a shoulder to cry on, I am here. I need to go now. Dealing with my friends, cousin and their shenanigans have left me totally pooped. Gonna call it a night now. Good night, Vivek." I smiled as brightly as I could, eager now to rush back to the room. Not before I was subjected to a toe-curling, butterfly-in-stomach-inducing loving, long, gentle look and a light stroke on the cheek.

"Good night, Oinks. See you in the morning. Thanks for this."

I walked back, almost floating in air, unable to comprehend what was going on? *Boy, what was that? Is he interested in me? Maybe, just maybe. It felt like. Or am I hallucinating and reading too much into this friendly gesture.*

These and many more not so appropriate thoughts were swirling and going about in my cluttered, messed-up mind when I entered the room. Where Sweety was waiting up for me to get back. It turned out that she had a lot on her mind – no, not about her and Divya's messed up scenario – but about me and my non-existent love-life.

"Where were you? Or should I ask whom were you with?" She hissed, keeping her voice a bit hushed, as her dear Divya was snoring gently beside her.

"Huh? With Vivek. Grabbing a drink. Why do you ask? I thought you would be asleep too." I replied, nonchalantly, shaking my head at the question. Typical of Sweety to assume the role of elder sister whenever she could.

God knows what got into her post my reply. Sweety frowned and forgetting Divya for a moment, she exclaimed,

"Vivek?? Why on earth would you be with him? Are you out of your mind?"

"Why not? He is an old friend..." I replied, not sure, where she was headed with this conversation.

"No, not him, Oinks. He caused you much heartbreak. It took you such a while to get back in shape. Now you are again flitting about around him. Also, I did not like him. He is not a reliable bloke."

"Wow, how did you gauge that? In 30 minutes? That he isn't reliable."

"Well, he doesn't remember Shreya. Wasn't that the name of your friend he dumped you for?"

"WHAT?? You asked him about Shreya? Come on, how could you? What did you even say to him?" Fuck. What had my irritating friend gone and blurted out? Why didn't he even mention that to me? I was now nearly furious. This interference, while expected, was super annoying.

"Hmm, not directly. I asked him about his school, where he studied, his friends, etc. Oh, he did mention that you had been classmates in school. Chill. Don't worry, I was kind of subtle."

Subtle, my bloody foot. Sweety did not do subtle. Period. She was Punjabi – what did she even know of subtlety?

"Coming back to the topic, Oinks, He is NOT the one for you. I may be biased and all. But I know this. He is like this false soulmate – one who mirrors a true soulmate but enters your life to cause pain and suffering only."

"Huh, false soulmate?" *What the fuck was that?*

"Yes, I heard about this concept from a psychic healer I visited last month," Sweety explained feeling and looking rather self-important!

WTF. Oh God, my friend had lost it. "Sweety, psychics? Healers? Why oh why? What is this new nonsense?"

"It isn't nonsense. She is good. Very good. Violet Dhingra is her name. Divya loved her."

Wonderful. Violet Dhingra is a lucky woman. She had after all been stamped with Divya's stamp of approval. I rolled my eyes and said, "Look, this is all a bloody hogwash. You and Divya wanna go, please do. Do spare me her phoney concepts though. False soulmate. Seriously?"

"You wanna believe or not, your wish. But Vivek isn't the guy for you. Especially now that there is Rajat." Sweety declared emphatically.

"Sweety is right… Yaaawn, Rajat is a good guy. I approve of him too," Divya added her two bits in her sleep, as she turned from one side to another.

"Oh good, darling, we will matchmake dear Oinks with Rajat tomorrow. We should do this to make up to her!" Sweety said, looking at a sleeping Divya.

I stared blankly at both. Sweety, who was on her own trip and didn't notice, and Divya, who was fast asleep wouldn't possibly notice. It was late in the evening and I was way too exhausted to react to these crazy women and their bombastic ideas. Honestly what do I even say? Together, the two of them were like the unstoppable forces of nature, unleashing their might in whichever direction they please; and unfortunately I was their latest target. Deciding to postpone the inevitable conflict (my will vs theirs – on so many matters and most importantly MY love life), I was all set to get some sleep. For maybe, these two ladies would jump on to yet another hare-brained scheme – affecting their love life and NOT my non-existent one. Tomorrow was after all another day.

24

And what a day, the next and the day after next, and the day after, the day after next turned out to be. Basically, the entire week during which Sweety and Divya had made my room their blessed abode was eventful. Memorable too – though that depended on whose perspective you saw it from.

If I had any hopes of them finding a new target, new mad cap plan, a new shenanigan to focus on, I was mistaken. From the time we got ready and went down for a leisurely (for them) and quick (for me) breakfast, they made it clear, painfully so, that I was to be their new project. As we sat down at the corner table, I noticed that Divya was more interested in looking around the restaurant than checking out the breakfast buffet. For Sweety, the first priority was always food. There she was, making a beeline for the food. "None of your colleagues are here yet." Divya said, surveying the place, almost disappointedly.

"No, they aren't. For all you know, they may have had breakfast by now. Have a meeting fairly early at the office of the CDPO. We are going on a tour of some *anganwadis* today."

Now Divya was least bit interested in where or what I did; so obviously this entire sentence of mine fell on deaf ears as she continued to look around. In order to appear plain fucking polite, I asked, "What are you both planning to do?

"Today or you mean, about life in general?"

"Both."

Divya looked at me with a rather fixed gaze. It looked like she was about to answer my question. But right at that very moment, she spotted someone behind me. Her face lit up. "Rajat, here, here, please come here." She beamed, as a bashful, yet pleased Rajat came and sat right next to me. "Hello Oindrilla, it is such a pleasure to meet you."

Hein? Had Rajat been kidnapped? Who was this alien in his place, impersonating him? Or was this his twin brother? More idiotic and irritating? The Rajat I knew used to be friendly and certainly not a simpering idiot.

Smiling a brief, perfunctory smile, I muttered some inane reply and promptly left to get some breakfast. It was then, on my way towards the buffet that I spotted Vivek enter, looking oh-so-lost-in-his-thoughts and dapper. Excitedly (a bit much I think), I waved at him, when I caught his eye and pointed him to the corner table. He smiled, a bit distractedly but nodded. Well, if I had to put up with Rajat's unwanted attentions, I would need some solace in the form of Vivek's pretty (well, not really!) visage. However, to my utter dismay, before Vivek could reach the corner table (when I was filling up my plate with an additional chocolate muffin), he was waylaid by the interfering Sweety. What she told him, I couldn't fathom from afar. Whatever she did, she managed to successfully veer him away from the corner table to another table in the opposite far end of the hall. I tried to get her attention, from this distance, using all the common signs we had perfected and used during our time together at university but the woman was steadfastly ignoring me. By this time, Aparna and Hawkeye had also arrived for breakfast and had taken their place at the corner table. This was extremely weird. What the hell was Sweety upto? And then it struck me. This was her and Divya's idiotic plan – to distract Vivek and keep him away from me; while pushing me towards Rajat! How exasperating! Did not these weird women get it? They may keep me away from Vivek at breakfast, lunch and dinner? What about the time when I would be at work with him? I was pissed when I saw through this juvenile game plan. Glaring at Divya who was seated across the corner table, I placed my plate and then sat down next to Rajat. Rajat perked up immediately and started fawning some more. *Fuck.* Had he not been a dear friend at some point in time, I would have socked him (after socking Sweety and Divya). However, one had to behave. So I did.

Breakfast turned out to be much of an ordeal. Hawkeye was unabashedly taken in with Divya, who made all the appropriate noises and gestures to convey interest. Rajat was trying hard to impress me; however, since I was not *daloing any ghaas* (and only staring at my phone), he entertained himself by talking to Aparna. Heaven knows, I never thought I would ever say it: but here goes. A frank admission – Aparna was the only sensible person on that table. Moreover, she noticed that I was being rather standoffish. At one point, when Rajat had excused himself, she quietly said to me, "What's the matter, Oindrilla? Have you and Rajat had a fallout of some sort? Thought you were friends."

"Hey, no nothing like that at all, Aparna. Am a bit preoccupied." I fibbed.

Not that she fell for it. "Umm, in case you need any tips to fend off unwanted attention, let me know. I should tell this to your friend, Divya as well." She said, in an oddly comforting manner, as she patted my hand.

Standoffish I was definitely being; not only to shoo Rajat and his unwanted attentions. The truth of the matter was that I was distracted. I was more interested in knowing what was happening at the other table where Sweety was clearly regaling Vivek with some jokes. Aparna, ever observant and ever present, commented a couple of times about the other table too. She wondered exactly what was going on. Sweety and Vivek were having a much better time than Divya, who was *jheloing* Hawkeye. Despite being ticked off rather openly by Aparna a couple of times, Hawkeye persisted in tormenting Divya.

While Rajat tried to get my attention and then went back into conversing with Aparna in the meantime, I kept staring at my phone or taking sneak peeks at Vivek. To my surprise, a couple of times I caught him staring at me as well (*Yay to that*).

While the 'not conversing on breakfast tables' had been my thing even in the past, being completely impolite and staring at phone in hand at the breakfast table was not. And that too to snub poor Rajat, whom I genuinely liked before he had turned into some weird, simpering lover boy. Poor guy, I didn't want him to get any ideas and was not looking forward to friend zoning him. *Blasted Sweety and Divya.* As if their lives were not complicated enough, they were hell bent on making a mess out of mine. Never before had I looked forward to my work day. A part of my irritation perhaps came on to my face, and a couple of times, I caught Aparna's gaze both perceptive and curious. At last, the blasted breakfast session, made miserable by my reticence and non interest in talking to Rajat and giving him any *bhaav*, finally got over. It was time for us colleagues to leave for the CDPO office.

"*He he he*, Oindrilla, now we have to bid adieu to your charming friends." Hawkeye who else? He seemed to be feeling the pangs of separation from Divya, a bit more than envisaged. Aparna and I had picked up our bags to head to the door. Rajat had stepped out, I suspect, for a quick smoke or a washroom break. Hawkeye was sitting still at it, unable to tear himself from Divya. By now, even she, patient she may have been, had a glazed look in her eyes. She needed to be rescued. Though her knight (ess) in shining armour was guffawing loudly at something Vivek had said.

I smiled at Hawkeye and turned away. The entire situation suddenly seemed hopelessly funny. And I was not the only one trying to stop my laughter. Even Aparna was struggling to hide her sheer amusement. Not surprising at all. While she did not know the entire complicated rigmarole that was playing out, her amusement was the result of Hawkeye's extremely gawkish behaviour. For all his irritating manners, the man was in reality a conservative, decent bloke. He was devoted to his wife and *bacchas*. While he was friendly, he never flirted with other women – his age or younger. Hence his being so taken in by Divya and subsequent behaviour like an idiotic schoolboy was strange and attention grabbing. We did not speak about it, Aparna and I, but both of us were thinking the same thing. The sooner Hawkeye headed back to Delhi the better.

"Aparna, when are you guys flying out?" I asked Aparna as we waited for Hawkeye, Rajat and Vivek in the hotel lobby a while later.

"Friday was the original plan. Got pushed to Saturday. Now however, I wonder whether I should suggest preponing. What do you say? How long are your friends here for?"

"Hmm, I have no idea about my friends. There is a bit of a complication there. Would it be possible to prepone?"

"Yeah. Let me speak to Boss and see if there can be an artificial emergency created in Delhi? The way Rahul is behaving, this won't end too pleasantly for him."

Over the course of that brief conversation, I had also gathered that Hawkeye's wife was a close friend of Aparna's. Hawkeye's behaviour was certainly none of my business. Whether he stayed put in Shillong or headed back to Delhi was his headache and somewhat Aparna's concern.

"By the way, don't mind my asking. Why are you ignoring Rajat, Oindrilla? I thought you were friends." Aparna asked me, as we waited.

"Uh oh. He is getting too friendly for my liking. Unwanted attention, you see. I wanna nip anything in the bud right away."

"Hmm, makes sense. Look, there they are. I will handle Rajat. You sit next to either Vivek or Rahul. Vivek is definitely the more pleasant option." Aparna smiled, first at me and then the approaching party. Among them, at Rajat in particular, whom she quietly engaged in some cock-a-doodle conversation.

"Oindrilla, Vivek, why don't you guys sit at the back please? I need to discuss something with Rajat." Aparna requested; sweetness personified. Rajat's face fell, while mine lit up.

25

The Innova cab ride to the CDPO office was uneventful. As ever, Hawkeye was schmoozing up to the driver. Rajat and Aparna were talking about something under the sun – Aparna doing the talking; and Rajat playing the reluctant listener. In the rear seat, it looked (to me, a biased me, a deluded me) that a whole new story was developing. With the newly restored camaraderie from last night (or the past few days), Vivek and I were rekindling our past equation – warm, friendly and extremely toe-curling. Almost as if we were picking up the threads from the good old school days – when we were rather close and all set to being an 'item', which would have happened but for a little hitch. The week leading to our farewell, I kept getting the feeling that Vivek was about to propose or suggest. Becoming an item, that is. I was hopeful that we would start dating. Or that's what the deluded 17 year old Oinks thought. However, a day before our school farewell, my then best friend Shreya excitedly came and told me that Vivek had asked her out on a date. Of course, I couldn't and didn't believe it at first. But my heart broke into a thousand smithereens that evening when I spotted them in the Starbucks on Park Street post our farewell. That was also the last I saw of him and Shreya.

In the cab, as we chatted about a whole lot of things, the weather, scenery and the upcoming project included, it felt like we had gone back in time. For a little while. You see, then all those painful, unpleasant memories came flooding back. I refused to be deluded and taken for a complete ride this time around. By the time we got off at the office, I was in a serious dilemma. Maybe Sweety was right. There was really no point in my getting involved in a screwed up one-sided equation. Again. Maybe I should pay more attention to Rajat.

It was this knee-jerk, impromptu volte-face that was to set the tone of the absolute confusion, which ensued over the next two days! Rajat got the shock, nay biggest surprise, of his life (*actually, so did I*) when I vociferously called out to him when we got down from the cab. Vivek looked stunned. But being the gentleman he was, and maybe because he had gotten dumped once before in real life, he did not seem to mind being dropped like a hot potato. As I dashed across to Rajat on an utterly nonsensical pretext, I heard Aparna ask Vivek, "What did you say to her? She was avoiding him earlier. Now she is running to him." Shit, it was only then that the height of my idiocy struck me. However, not much could be done. Rajat, thrilled at this unexpected attention, turned all gooey, idiotic and charming. *SUFFER, OINKS, SUFFER! You deserve this.*

The rest of the work day passed in a tizzy. For one, there were quite a few meetings planned. First half of the day was to be spent chalking out the details of the technological implementation. The Integrated Child Development Scheme (ICDS) officials were keen on understanding how the software worked. It was such a relief to see Rajat back in his professional avatar – the gooey, mushy lover-boy type was getting on my nerves. As if in competition, at least it seemed to me and my extremely juvenile self, Vivek, was also in his element. I had never seen him make a presentation before – naturally, the previous time I had seen him kind of on stage was during an intra-school debate competition! His slow and deliberate enunciation of the project plan and the laying of details in clear, concise terms was several notches above that performance in the school debate. *Idiot. What a comparison!* Nevertheless, both the men were charming and at one point of time, during a typically distracted moment, I found myself evaluating and comparing the two men. Much to my own horror. *Oindrilla Roy, get back to your bloody senses. No. 1: Spending a night with Sweety and Divya did not mean that you lose your mind and start behaving like them.*

No. 2: Your idiocy has already complicated matters. Rajat, a decent guy who likes you, thinks you do like him too and that you are leading him on. Vivek, whom you really really like and have liked since time immemorial, thinks you are leading Rajat on, after sending him blow-hot-blow-cold signals continuously since the past few days. And now, to complicate matters, you are pitting them one against the other. Either way, you will be solely responsible for hurting one of these decent guys.

So BEHAVE!

***

This line of thought therefore was discarded and I forced myself to concentrate on work. The second half of the day would hopefully ensure that. For visits to three *anganwadis* – Madan Ingsyiem A, Madan Ingsyiem B, and Mawsawa had been planned. In my pre-Shillong life, I used to thoroughly enjoy field trips, especially visits to the *anganwadis*, where I spent time with the children, the *anganwadi* helpers, *anganwadi* workers, the didis, listening to their stories, collecting data for my future research, etc. The afternoon session was what I was looking forward to. It also meant that I did not have even a moment to waste thinking of past or future romantic encounters – with the old could-have-been-beau or the friend itching to be new beau. Not that it meant much. My impulsive action earlier in the day had left its mark.

Rajat was constantly hovering around me. Aargh. A single free moment, and he was right beside me, smiling and attentive. On the other hand, Vivek was totally shunning me. A couple of times, when I looked up midway during one of the meetings, I did spot him looking at me (hurt and anguished – which was purely my interpretation, and hence suspect) but he looked away immediately. *What was I to expect? Run from him like that and drop him like a hot potato and he will still hover around you?* Twice, I tried to make small talk with him. Partly out of guilt at my own inexplicable behaviour which may have caused him some grief. *You idiot. Grief or not, it was loss of face. What would have Aparna thought?* Small mercy that Hawkeye was busy trying to wheedle some info out of the taciturn Mr Norbhum, who turned out to be our Innova driver for the second day in a row! Had he witnessed this episode I would have been ragged endlessly.

Both times, maybe because my efforts at approaching him were half-hearted, or maybe because he had been slighted, he wasn't particularly friendly. Formal, cold, and distant – gone was my friend/crush or whatever Vivek, the boy I knew from school and in his place was this professional, and exacting to the bloody point.

By the time we got done with the day, I was bugged. More with myself. And then with simpering Rajat. Who was acting like he was my protector, friend, pet lamb all rolled-in-one. Not only was he hanging on to every word I said (to just about anyone), he also kept handing my water/coffee/a chair to sit where ever I went. *Aargh*. Twice at the Mawsawa *anganwadi*, I almost came close to whacking him. Much to Vivek's amusement. This was when he handed me yet another glass of water, when I was interacting with some of the children.

"What now, Rajat?" I snapped, as Rajat handed me a glass of warm water, with a beatific smile on his face. "I didn't ask for it, did I?"

"Oindrilla, you coughed. You are straining your throat."

WTF. This was bloody annoying. In front of the kids, Aparna and a smirking Vivek, I couldn't do much but to accept this glass of water offered to me on a platter as graciously as I could. This was to be just the beginning – a little while later, he even offered me his hand as I was getting up. Good Lord, it took me a great ounce of patience and forbearance to stop myself from blasting him and giving an earful. Something which Vivek noticed and smirked, despite his cold demeanour towards me (much to my excitement). No, this wasn't me being delusional and assuming. But when Rajat was patiently demonstrating the technology and software to the ICDS officials present with us (*Phew, at least this made me remember that this man had a profession, which he was damn good at*), Vivek and I were seated at the far end of the room. "Oinks, good job. You are doing well trying to restrain yourself."

"I beg your pardon. What do you mean?"

"Don't pretend! You know very well what I mean. If you want me to spell it out. Twice, you have come close to lashing out at your newly adopted pet," Vivek said, rather sardonically.

"Pet? Come on, Rajat is not my pet."

"He certainly is behaving like your little lamb."

"No, not at all. He isn't. Don't be mean, Vivek." Considering I had brought Rajat's unwanted attentions entirely upon myself, I felt a sudden need to defend him. That and because he was a friend. Though an irritating one, at the moment. But still a friend.

"If you say so. By the way, care to explain, what exactly prompted your actions this morning?"

Uh oh, I hadn't seen that coming. Considering I was like an ostrich most of the time, that is I ducked my head the moment I saw any sign of conflict or trouble or confrontation, I had but conceitedly assumed everyone to be so; Vivek included. Hence this direct question targeted at me asking me for an explanation was unexpected and a bit much to handle.

I hemmed and hawed for a minute, uncomfortably, looking here, there and everywhere. Since I knew not what to say to Vivek – I couldn't blurt out that I ran to Rajat to stop falling in love with him – and having spotted Aparna enter the room (she had stepped out to make a few phone calls to the media guys), I scooted, after mouthing some far-fetched excuse.

"Running away, as usual, Oinks." I heard Vivek mutter, as I fled.

To avoid any further embarrassing moments, I steered clear of Vivek (whose demeanour had turned dark and dreary) and tried hard (unsuccessfully) to get Rajat off my back.

26

By the time we got back to Rosewood Hotel that evening, I was done with myself, with Rajat and most importantly the idiotic Sweety-Divya duo. Speaking of them, I wondered what they had been up to. No, not on my own. It was because, as we neared the hotel, I suspect that Hawkeye remembered Divya. Taking a break from his one-sided monologue with (now harassed looking) Norbhum, he looked back and said, "*Arre*, Oindrilla, what have your dear friends been up to?"

How the fuck was I supposed to know? I was there, with Hawkeye and the others, attending painful meetings. No, no I wasn't that much of a dodo to blurt that out. Instead, I politely muttered, "Not sure, haven't checked with them."

"*Arre, arree, aise kaise,* check *karo*."

I looked at Aparna, who was also rolling her eyes like me at Hawkeye's desperate behaviour. He needed to be sent back to Delhi. For all of EOFA's irksome issues, indecency and lack of decorum has not been one of them. Primarily because the Big Boss is one staunch temple-going, curd-rice eating Tambrahm. You may wonder what that had to do with the overall moral standards of the place. The thing is that he insisted on hiring decent people. He had on board a private detective agency that profiled and did a proper, thorough check on any potential employee. Hawkeye was a decent bloke, a committed husband, doting dad, etc. Hence this weird (teenager-ish) behaviour of Hawkeye was surprising.

"Aparna, what do we do about him?" I whispered, rather softly.

She didn't reply instead she whipped out her phone and shot me a message. Easier way to communicate if the topic was a little indiscreet!

"Under control. Hawkeye leaves tomorrow. I called Vikram."

I looked up in horror. Vikram was HR. Had Aparna complained? She understood my dying duck-like expression and replied.

"Don't be silly. Not a complaint. Vikram is this guy's best friend. He said he would concoct some crisis by evening."

Phew. As if on cue, Hawkeye got a call and it was Vikram. Going by Hawkeye's rather deflated expression, it was clear. Aparna's idea had worked. After the call, he announced, sadly that he had to leave the next afternoon along with Aparna and Rajat.

Rajat looked surprised. Well, so did I. And even Aparna.

A: This wasn't part of the plan.

Me: Oh. Let's see what happens.

Aparna smiled and said to Hawkeye, "Rahul, I get it, you and I need to head back. But isn't Rajat required here?"

"Naa, Oindrilla knows enough about the software to take care of this project." Hawkeye's faith in me was rather touching. I was indeed familiar with the software and could expertly handle any queries – as long as they were not related to its code.

Rajat, being the maker-shaker would be required for any dire situation.

I nodded and added, "Rahul, I can handle basic queries, yes. What if something goes wrong?"

"We will see then. There is a new project opportunity; one that has come up today. In Haryana, Karnal, I think. Boss will be presenting in a few days. He thinks Rajat is required there. So Rajat, off we go tomorrow."

"Sure, Rahul."

One major thing this guaranteed was that Hawkeye now had no time to fawn over Divya. He had some stuff to take care of before his flight the next afternoon, sending him into a work mode tizzy. Yay! This also meant that I no longer had to desperately call Sweety and Divya (at his behest) to find out where they were. Divya was spared. And so was I. I deluded myself into thinking that Rajat would also now have no time to spare any attention towards me. It was soon proved, how wrong I was.

For I was waylaid by Rajat on my way to the elevator lobby at the hotel (when we got there), who asked me if I could have a cup of tea with him in the café. Considering that he was looking green and a bit uncomfortable and I was longing for some caffeine too, I agreed. Much to my own chagrin. This coffee date, if you may, was to be one of the most painful ever. How difficult would it be to stuff myself with a cookie or brownie and coffee and converse with Rajat? Normally, not at all. But for my brilliant 'leading him on' this morning (*of course, you bloody idiot, all your fault for flying to him, squealing Oh Rajat!*), it would have been a friendly conversation. But something had changed. Barely had I bit into my luscious, yummy, chocolatey pastry, did he clear his throat and began, "Oindrilla, I have been struggling today."

"Oh, so sorry. What happened, Rajat? I thought the demo and presentation went well."

He looked at me, a little confused, and then replied, "Oh it did. I am not referring to that."

"Oh dear, are you coming down with some kind of a flu or viral fever?"

"No, no, not at all." He put down his cup of coffee and put his hand over mine. YIKES!

"My feelings. I have been struggling with them. I like you. Maybe we should date."

Aaargh no no no! I stared at him, for eternity, with a shocked dying duck expression. Not a word came out.

Seeing that as an encouragement, he added, "I was looking forward to this Shillong trip as I had texted you. But then I wasn't sure of my feelings. You know how things have been for me since my break-up. You are funny, sweet, friendly. I do like you."

FUCK. What had I gotten myself into?

Finally sense dawned on me and I replied; else before I knew it, I would have gotten engaged and worse hitched at this rate!

"Rajat, this is a bit sudden." *Such a liar, you are, Oindrilla Roy!* "I don't know what to say. I am sorry. I like you, very much but not in that sense. You are a friend. I may have given you some wrong ideas perhaps. Sorry but that wasn't my intention. Besides, you are still smarting from what happened with Shilpa. Sorry." I patted his hand and then scooted back to my room. Feeling utterly bugged and miserable. And it was all thanks to my idiotic friend and her partner, who, at that very moment, were plonked on the couch and watching a rerun of *My Best Friend's Wedding* for the nth time on the television. In my room. I barged in to find them giggling. And that made me feel worse.

"Hey, what happened, girl? You don't look good. As if you are about to cry!" Divya said, observant as ever. Sweety, who knew me better, shushed Divya and added, "Are you angry about something?"

"Yes, you both. Thanks to your idiotic counselling, I am in a mess. Rajat proposed. I refused him, Vivek hates me. I love him. Even now. I hate my fucking *tatti* life and want to go back to feed my *kuttas* back home!" I flung myself on to the bed and started sobbing. This whole situation had gotten to me.

Sweety came over to the bed and patted me on my back as I continued to wail and sob. After what seemed like an eternity, I stopped. A good cry did wonders. Always. It felt so good. Divya handed me a glass of water and then sat in front of me. It was indeed time to sort out the entire mess.

"Feeling better? Now, what happened?" It was Divya, being the voice of reason. In as much detail as I could remember, I told them what happened. Most of which they knew already. Divya looked at Sweety, after which Sweety sheepishly began.

"Hey, sorry, ya. Oinks, Divya and I had a long heart-to-heart and we discussed everything under the sun. Our relationship, future and also what we had been trying to do to you. Sorry. We shouldn't have meddled."

I looked at Sweety blankly. Whenever Sweety got serious, it meant it was bloody serious.

"What is going on?"

Divya now added. "Look, we have decided to head back tomorrow. This whole elopement bit was knee-jerk and you were right in being annoyed with us. While I knew what we were doing was wrong, your disapproval and plain speaking helped. I plan to go home and tell my folks that I am in love with Sweety and I am not interested in *shaadi* and all. Once we do that, we will need all your support."

Oh, suddenly I felt so much better. "This is great. I am happy for you. Though Delhi will be in a state of uproar. I can already expect Ma calling me to check whether I have a girlfriend hidden away somewhere here. She may even land up here." I chuckled and gave them both a big, warm hug. Maybe Divya wasn't so bad after all – despite her superciliousness and bitchiness. Oh well, she was the South Delhi type – couldn't help it, could she?

Sweety cleared her throat. The discussion was not over. "Also, I am sorry for telling you to go and focus on Rajat. I never thought you would listen to me though. You never have."

"Hmm, I usually don't listen to anyone. I don't know why I did. Or maybe I do. You see, I think I am still in love with Vivek. Am I not pathetic?" I flung myself, this time, into Sweety's arms and wailed some more.

Divya said, "Ok, I don't see what the problem is. Sorry. He is nice, here, and available. Didn't he get dumped or dump his fiancé or some such thing? Go and tell him what you feel? What's the most that can go wrong?" Sweety seemed to agree to Divya's suggestion.

I stared at Divya. She made perfect sense. I had anyway made an ass of myself so many times. Maybe this was worth a try. I nodded, and before better sense and second thoughts could enter my head, Sweety handed me my phone. "Call him."

"No no, I am not calling him!" And before I completely chickened out on this idea, I was seized by a crazy impulse, I took the phone and sent him a message instead. With both the women eagerly watching what I typed.

Me: Hey, you free? I need to talk.

V: Yes, you can call now.

Me: No, can I come over?

V: Hmm, ok...

"Go now," Sweety squealed excitedly. Divya stopped me and took a critical look at my face. "No, go wash your face first." After 10 minutes and a *hazaar* pep talks (all within that time), I gathered all my courage and went up to face Vivek, who was still not happy with me and my behaviour and made it evidently clear, when he opened his room door. *Shit. Fuck. I wanted to go back. This felt like a disaster. No, Oindrilla Roy. Own up. The worst that will happen is that he will break your heart. You know how that feels! You lived back then. You will continue to live now.*

I entered the room, and since I could not find anything better to say, I blurted the most silly thing that came to my head. "Nice light."

"What?" He looked at me as if I had lost my head. "Oinks, what's the matter? You surely have not come here to comment on the room décor, which incidentally is the same as your room."

I shook my head. "Can I have a glass of water?"

The cold Vivek was immediately replaced by the normal, gentle Vivek. For this was so unlike me.

"Are you okay? No, you don't seem fine. What happened?"

He handed me a glass of water and gently took my hand and led me to the couch.

"I am ok, kind of. But not really. This couch is so soft. And colourful." (*Brilliant. It is amazing how coherence completely leaves me and my idiotic self, whenever I am faced with uncomfortable situations.*)

"Oinks, now will you please tell me what is going on?"

And before, just before I lose my slowly fading, ebbing confidence, I blurt out, "Vivek, I think I am in love with you..." Vivek looked stunned. He certainly hadn't anticipated that! He didn't say a word, for what seemed to me like eternity.

Oh fuck. Damn you Sweety. What the hell had I done? Barely had those words come out of my mouth, mortification set in. I wanted to sink right through the ground – like Sita. But since that was not to happen, I decided to do the next best thing. Get up and bolt.

Now instead of going back to my room, which was a mere two doors away, I ran towards the stairs – hoping to calm my rapidly beating mortified heart and get some cool air. I was by the emergency exit door leading to the staircase, when I heard him.

"Wait. Stop. Now don't you disappear for the next ten years, Oinks," Vivek had recovered from whatever shock my words may or may not have subjected him to – the smirk on his face made it clear.

Sweety, Divya – I am going to kill you both.

"Ok. What is it? Vivek?" I squawked with as much confidence I could muster, looking up at him. *Good lord. Can I just die?*

Vivek didn't say a thing. He was standing just a foot away from me, looking rather constipated. Poor guy, I threw him such a googly.

To my absolute shock (and thrill), he came close to me and placed his arm on my shoulder and looked me deep in the eye, and pulled me closer. "Oinks, what do you mean you think you love me?"

I shut my eyes – to escape this inevitable interrogation.

"Err, err, I think I love you. Maybe I don't. But I like you very much. That I have and then Sweety thought I should…" I find myself being shushed. *Thank god, he had the sense to shut my blabbering self.* "Shush. You may not be sure. Know that I am in love with you. I may have been for a while." And before I could think or say anything, Vivek Rao kissed me. Softly, deeply, gently.

Epilogue – A few months later

Who would have thought that *seedha-saadha* Vivek Rao would turn out to be such a hot kisser and an even better lover. (Well, I am certainly not spilling the details.) But my *tatti* life became infinitely better since that sexy moment. The months I spent at Shillong (with Vivek) on that project were amazing. I have been less grumpy, more sociable and generally happy. Why, now that the project is over and I am back in Delhi, I am even looking at those damn dogs more fondly.

Things have changed. After her scarring experience, Ankita decided to go abroad and study further. She wants nothing to do with Naxalite men or any man as such. After acing her GRE, as of next month, she is shifting to the US. Sweety and Divya made their explosive revelation at their respective homes and to their shock (and mine), it was well-received. Sweety's mom, apparently, had an inkling from before and had prepared everyone else for it. Ma's reaction was exactly what I predicted. She freaked out and landed up in Shillong without letting me know and walked in on me at an extremely inopportune moment. She caught me smooching Vivek. To our utter surprise, instead of throwing a fit and whacking us and doing whatever parents do in such situations, she was super thrilled and she hugged us both! You see, she thought, I was also like Sweety. Seeing me kiss a hot-bodied male was such a relief that she couldn't contain her joy. What transpired however is that Vivek and I were bulldozed into making this official. He didn't seem to mind. I did. I had no chance of backing away now.

Vivek and I are getting engaged next week.

Acknowledgements

A conversation in a fifth-floor office in South Delhi, one April afternoon in 2018 triggered this book. My then-colleague and now friend, Aikantika Das had just finished recounting a particularly funny incident. As I laughed, I remember telling her that this incident deserves to go into a book. She smiled and in her typical nonchalant way said, "Go ahead, write about that. I do not care!" And that day I started writing *The Ex Factor*. Countless drafts and many revisions later, while the story has changed its shape and size – the incident still is a part of it. Thank you, Aikantika – you have been such a sport about this whole thing.

Shantanu Ray Chaudhari – I am grateful to you for believing in this story; at a time when I had given up all hope of seeing this published. Thank you.

I would also like to acknowledge the support of the entire Om Books team – the publisher Ajay Mago, for being gracious in accepting my story, my editor Sheela Roy, for polishing the rough edges, Soumya Duggal, for her painstaking efforts in ironing out the proofs, the marketing & PR manager, Ruchika Khanna, for trusting the subject and everyone else involved in the book. My heartfelt thanks to Ananya Saha for her insights. Kiran Manral – Thank you. You have always been so kind and encouraging. You are an inspiration.

I am grateful to my dear friends – Priyanka Sondur, Kanchana Banerjee, Liji Narayan, Harprit Kaur, Kanchan Gupta, Angel Sivan, Manisha Kalaver, Deepa Pant and Maithili Sinha – for always having my back.

Tilottama Mukherjee – thank you for all your love and encouragement. Frederick Roy Kharkhongor – thank you for all the conversations, discussions & support.

Last but not the least, I would like to acknowledge with gratitude, love, and support of my family – my parents, my sister, Malini; my brother, Srirangan; my son, Nigamanth; and my husband, Vinod. My utmost gratitude to my Guruji for his blessings always.